Helter Skelter

Tales of Horror

Bryan Cassiday

Library of Congress Control Number:
2011908972
ISBN 978-0-983498933
Bryan Cassiday
Los Angeles

Printed in the United States of America
Second Edition: May 2012

Contents

The Dead of the Night

5

Lamia

18

It's for You

47

The Green Parrot

55

Blindman's Buff

72

Room 208

84

Black Dog

100

The Undertaker

115

Shambles

136

Kiss of Death

154

Snakebit
168
Confessions from the Grave
181
The Invisible Enemy
196

The Dead of the Night

A man had torn out the throat of my next-door neighbor last night.

Nobody had heard a sound. The murder victim was an old woman with a wrinkled face like a walnut. She had a cast to one of her blue eyes. She once told me she had great difficulty reading the walk signal at the traffic intersection at the corner of our block. She wore spectacles, but they afforded her little help. She told me she was ninety-two.

That same night a zombie had taken a bite out of my arm . . .

I had been sleeping when I felt tremendous pain in my forearm. The shock of the pain woke me up. I jackknifed upright in my bed.

A man with a ghoul's face was standing over me, blood dripping from his lips. I shoved him away from me. He came back at me. I hauled off and punched him spang in the nose. I thought I heard his nose crack. Whatever it was that cracked, he didn't like the pain it caused. He groaned. He left my room after that. Could fragments of the bone in his nose have penetrated his brain on account of my blow?

I could not figure out how he had gotten into my apartment. Hadn't I locked my door before I had gone to bed? I thought I always did. Locking the door was part of my nightly ritual. For the life of me I could not remember. I realized my arm was bleeding all over my sheets.

I bolted to the bathroom to retrieve a towel. I wrapped the towel around my wounded forearm to stanch the bleeding. Apprehensively, I wondered if the zombie had infected me with his bite. From movies, I knew that if a zombie bit you, you were doomed to turn into a zombie yourself. How much longer did I have to live? The idea of turning into a zombie mortified me.

Should I go to a doctor? What good would a doctor do? After all, doctors could not cure a zombie bite. If I was, indeed, contaminated by the zombie germs, it was only a matter of time before I became a zombie.

I took two Tylenols to kill the pain in my throbbing arm. I looked at the towel wrapped around my arm. I didn't see any blood. Perhaps my wound had stopped bleeding. That was a good sign.

I closed my apartment door, which the zombie had left open when he had departed. I decided to go back to sleep. Easier said than done. I tossed and turned the entire night. I kept worrying about whether I should have gone to a doctor. I sweated bullets wondering how long it would take for me to morph into a zombie. The buzzing of the refrigerator in the kitchen kept me awake. The sound seemed inordinately loud for some reason. At last I managed to drift off just before sunrise.

The murder victim's daughter jerked me awake with her shriek the next morning. I figured I was lucky if I had got about an hour's sleep all told during the night. I jumped out of bed.

I crossed the hall to the old woman's apartment. Everybody in the apartment house was constellating around her doorway. The daughter phoned the police. I recognized a few of the spectators around the doorway. They all lived near me, yet I knew only two of them on sight.

I did recognize the skinny sixtysomething woman with the black poodle. The woman was nervously smoking a long cigarette. Ash fell like rain from her bony fingers. She went everywhere with her poodle, I knew. The poodle wore a different-colored ribbon around his neck every day.

Standing near us a fortyish woman clad in a white terrycloth bathrobe and a pink plastic shower cap coughed. "You're not allowed to smoke in the hall," she chided her.

"Oh, I forgot I was smoking," said the woman with the poodle. "I ran out of my room so fast when I heard the scream I forgot to put out my cigarette."

She cast around for a wastebasket for the cigarette. She couldn't find one. She decided to snuff out the cigarette with her fingers and keep holding it for lack of anything else to do with it.

The woman in the bathrobe shuffled away from us in her mules.

"That woman is so mean," the woman with the poodle confided to me.

"Yes," I agreed.

"What happened to your arm?" she asked me, noticing the towel wrapped around it.

"It's just a cut," I said.

I didn't want to tell anyone about the zombie's attacking me. As far as I was concerned, it was nobody's business. The information would only serve to panic everybody. What good would that do?

"Did you hear any suspicious noises last night?" she asked.

"No."

"Neither did I. This is all very strange. Why didn't anyone hear the murderer?"

The police arrived.

All of the residents in the apartment house were scared. They asked the police how they could prevent the killer from entering their apartments. The police told them to make certain they secured the deadbolt locks in their apartments. Some of the residents decided they would buy guns.

The world was going crazy, I decided. One of my neighbors had had her throat torn out last night and I had been attacked by a zombie. What next? Why hadn't the zombie attacked anyone else? Maybe I had injured it so severely with my blow to its nose that it didn't have a chance to assault anyone else. Maybe it had wandered off somewhere and died for real this time. I wondered if it was the zombie that had torn out the old woman's throat.

I sat in my room all day. I called in sick. I didn't go to my job at the Los Angeles Public Library. My wounded arm was bothering me. I felt ill. I would be no use sorting library books today. I stared at the walls in my apartment. It was depressing. I told myself I needed to go to a doctor and have him examine my arm. I decided against it. The doctor would never believe me if I told him a zombie had bitten me.

I didn't know what to do with myself. I looked out my window. I watched the children riding their bicycles with raised handlebars on the sidewalk below. Cars sped past them indifferently down the pavement under the overcast dingy sky.

I wanted to forget everything. I especially wanted to forget last night.

I watched a bald black man scrounge through a public wastebasket on the sidewalk. He hauled out newspapers from the wastebasket. He collected more newspapers in another trash basket a block away. He would probably take them to the recycling center to collect money for them. I used to catch him rummaging through the garbage in our apartment house's Dumpster in the garage.

The white sun glittered like a cat's eye through the shifting eucalyptus leaves above my grime-streaked window. The eucalyptus tree was growing out of the sidewalk in front of my apartment house. The tree was dying, but the city hadn't decided to cut it down yet. The leaves clicked in the wind like a deck of cards being shuffled. I felt the wind wafting across my arm. I withdrew from the window. I paced the room for a while.

I finally decided to read a book. I chose a mystery I had checked out from the library. I liked mysteries because everything was neatly ordered. Mystery novels imparted to my mind the meaning and significance my life lacked. Every event in a mystery added up to a logical conclusion.

Sometimes I read philosophy books, but I doubted their validity. It was as though philosophers never looked beyond the printed word. Mystery novels made sense to me. They provided my mind with the pattern it needed to see in life. Philosophy, on the other hand, made me skeptical.

I sat on my bed and fell to reading the latest Lee Child mystery thriller.

I eventually got through the day. I cooked a frozen fried chicken TV dinner. I watched the TV news. I wrapped my wounded arm with a fresh bandage.

My mother called me. I answered the phone. She wanted to know what I was doing. I told her I wasn't doing anything. She asked me if I was OK. I said yes. What was I going to tell her? That a zombie bit me? We chatted for a while. We hung up.

I went to sleep.

A man entered my apartment through the kitchen window. How could he? My apartment was on the fourth floor. Did he bring a ladder? His black skulking shape thrust through the beige monk's cloth drapes into my kitchen.

I gazed in frozen horror at him from my bed. Was it the zombie? I could not tell. It was too dark. Did he see me? He charged through the room in a hunching posture like a bull. I could not discern his features. I could distinguish only a black silhouette. I didn't know what to do. If only I owned a pistol!

He hurled his massive bulk onto my chest. I stopped breathing. I attempted to buck him off me.

I could not move my hands! They seemed paralyzed at my sides. I could not even clench a fist. The intruder's sudden onslaught of weight knocked the wind out of me. I felt his colossal hands wringing my neck. I wanted to scream. I barely managed to open my mouth. I could not scream! I tried. Oh, how I tried! For the life of me, I could not scream. Not a word, not a breath passed my lips.

My eyes burst out of my head in terror. I tried again to move my hands. I could not move a muscle. I tried to breathe. I could not breathe.

I lay paralyzed under the killer's crushing weight. His hands collared my neck, digging deeper into my throat, cutting off my air. Yet I didn't die. I seemed to lie like this for hours. I could not breathe, yet I could not die.

I awoke the next morning to the sound of a police siren. Logy, I flung on a bathrobe. I left my apartment. A gaggle of apartment dwellers clustered in front of a resident's door down the hall. I wandered toward them.

"What happened?" I asked the woman with the poodle.

"Another woman had her throat torn apart," she said in shock.

Three policeman tramped down the corridor to the murder scene.

I retreated toward my apartment. The woman and her poodle accompanied me. I had known the woman casually for a year. Yet I still didn't know her name.

"Isn't it awful?" she said.

"Somebody broke into my room last night," I said.

"Oh no," she gasped.

Even her poodle looked nonplussed. He was wearing a pink ribbon today, I noticed.

"He tried to kill me," I said.

"It must have been the same man who killed Mrs. Chauncy and Mrs. Rhinegold."

She eyed me in consternation. Fright condensed into tears in her eyes.

"I don't know how I survived," I said distantly. "I couldn't breathe. I thought I was dead."

"How did you get away from him?"

"I don't know."

"You must have fought him off."

"I must have."

"Oh my God. Who'll be next? That's all we need in this world: another madman. As if the world wasn't crazy enough as it is."

"I can't understand why he let me live."

"Nobody can understand a madman."

I felt relieved that she agreed with me about the madman's incomprehensible motives.

I retuned to my apartment. She tottered down the hall. She always looked as though she was about to topple to the ground.

I surveyed my apartment. Nothing looked out of place. Why had the intruder jumped me? Why had he released me? Had he assailed me by mistake? Perhaps he thought I was Mrs. Rhinegold and when he realized his error he fled. Why did he murder Mrs. Rhinegold and Mrs. Chauncy? I became apprehensive. What if the killer came to the conclusion now that he must murder me because he thought I could identify him as the killer of the two women?

I decided to buy a gun.

I drove to a gun shop near the beach in Santa Monica. I talked to the barrel-chested owner. He was wearing a yellow baseball cap with its bill tilted upward. I told him I wanted to buy a revolver. We discussed the details in muted conspiratorial voices.

"Why do you want a revolver?" he asked as though I had committed a crime.

His brown eyes bored into my head. His bushy black eyebrows screened the upper half of his eyes. He seemed to be peering at me from under Spanish moss.

"I need it for self-protection," I answered. "There's a killer roaming around in my apartment house."

"Why not an automatic? I have a nice 9 mm Beretta here. Great stopping power."

He withdrew a black automatic from the glass display case in front of him. He held up the pistol admiringly for me to inspect it.

"Isn't there a holding period before I can take this gun home?" I asked.

"Not unless you want there to be." He winked at me.

I bought the Beretta and clips of ammunition for it with a credit card, hopefully not maxing out my credit line.

I studied the gun in my apartment. I wondered if I could actually kill another human being. On the face of it, murder was easy. Killing a human being merely required a squeeze of the trigger. The bullet punctured the delicate flesh, and that was the end of a two-legged creature. Only a reed, but a thinking reed—as the philosopher Pascal had called man.

The question was, would I live long enough to confront the murderer? Or would the zombie's bite finish me off before then?

I loaded a magazine into the automatic's butt. I slid the pistol into the top drawer of the bureau beside the head of my bed. I reclined in the only chair I possessed. I waited for the night.

Every time I heard footfalls down the corridor I reached anxiously toward my bureau's top drawer. I consoled myself that I had no reason to worry, since the murderer attacked only in the dead of the night.

I flicked the TV set on but paid no attention to it. I tried to read. I could not concentrate. I kept thinking about the killer. I felt edgy. I knew my neighbors felt the same way.

The apartment house sounded unnaturally quiet, as if all the residents were waiting in dread for the killer to strike again. Footsteps through the corridor seemed hastened. The dwellers dared not spend any more time than necessary out of their apartments.

A neighbor who inveterately whistled popular tunes set to whistling softly in his room. He could not carry the tune. He ceased. The eerie silence racked my twitching nerves.

I realized it was all pointless. None of it mattered. So what if the killer wasted me tonight? I looked at my bandaged arm. I had been bitten by a zombie. I had no future. I had nothing. Let the killer rip out my throat. Death would release me from the unbearable wretchedness of having to wait to turn into a zombie. I felt impotent. I was convinced I would turn into a zombie any time now. Death would be preferable to being one of the living dead. Then I wondered: would I still turn into a zombie if I died not because of the zombie bite but because of a severed throat?

I had reached the point now where my intellect didn't care one way or the other whether I lived or died. Why worry?

I relaxed.

I recollected the theory that everyone got exactly what he wanted in this world. Murder victims wanted to get murdered. Didn't Dostoyevsky say that? I found his theory hard to swallow. Did all of us actually crave pain and misery? Did a double amputee secretly desire to lose two limbs? You could probably justify everything if you thought about it long enough. By the same token you could condemn everything.

I felt tired of thinking. Thinking tied my brain into a Gordian knot. If I thought too much I could not unfasten the knot. *Thinking sucks!*

I realized I was famished. I succumbed to an overpowering urge to consume meat. I strode to the refrigerator in the kitchenette, yanked open the refrigerator door, drew open the white plastic meat drawer, and snapped up a package of fresh ground round.

My mouth watered as I scoped out the beef. I ripped off the package's shrink-wrap, scooped out a large red clump of ground beef with my hand, and stuffed the beef into my mouth. I groaned with delight.

I could not believe how succulent the raw meat tasted. In a trice I gobbled down the rest of the beef and tossed its empty Styrofoam package onto the kitchenette's linoleum tiles.

I had never felt that hungry before in my life. I licked my lips with delight.

But then I felt sick. I thought I was going to retch. What the hell had I been thinking? Why did I eat raw meat for Christ's sake?

Feeling nauseous I angled toward the bathroom. I experienced difficulty moving my legs. Maybe my nausea was affecting my coordination. I skittered rather than walked into the bathroom.

I stood in front of the mirror and, in disgust, winced at my reflection in it. *Christ, I look like shit!* My face appeared drawn and ashen. My complexion had taken on a faint greenish hue the color of veins. Just looking at my face was enough to make me want to puke. Not even my mother would love this face. I caught myself snickering. What did I think was so funny? I asked myself.

I was having trouble maintaining my balance. Lightheaded, I braced my hands on the porcelain sink.

Maybe I had gorged on the raw meat because I was anemic. Perhaps I had lost too much blood from my wound. I decided I needed to sleep.

Collecting myself after a fashion, I tried to brush my teeth in front of the toothpaste-splattered mirror. It seemed unbelievably difficult just to guide the brush into my mouth. I finally had to give up. I dropped the brush into the sink in defeat. It was obvious I was too beat to do anything.

I retreated to my bed. I made a hash of undressing. I climbed into bed, more like fell into it, and drifted off into a kind of sleepless limbo.

The drapes billowed into my room. A black hulking shape thudded against the carpet. My mind flared into consciousness. Frantically, I devised my defense. I remembered the loaded pistol. I had to reach it. My arm felt palsied at my side. Petrified with fear, I watched the killer stride headlong toward me. I had to reach my pistol! I strained to extend my hand toward the bureau. I balked, my mind and body disjoined.

He leapt onto me. He straddled my chest. As before, he suffocated me with his massive weight. I tried to move. I could not move. I tried to scream. I could not. He throttled me with his gnarled, powerful hands. Like burning sulfur a scream caught in my throat.

I became conscious of a throbbing headache. Footsteps clamored down the corridor outside my apartment's door.

"She's dead!" a woman screamed. "The madman tore out her throat and her poodle's!"

My hand was perspiring. Something lay in it. My pistol? I glanced at my hand dangling over the edge of the bed. A bloodstained pink ribbon tied in a crumpled bow was nestled in my bloody palm.

With revulsion I realized my crime.

I looked at my bandaged arm. Was I already a zombie? Had I become a zombie the instant I had been bitten?

I felt nothing. My headache seemed to vanish. I tasted a scrumptious warm metallic-tasting fluid in my mouth. I swallowed the fluid with relish and wished I could drink more of it. I wiped a drop of it off the corner of my mouth and examined the back of my hand. The fluid was blood.

On my back I gazed from my bed at the paint that was peeling from my ceiling. In a flash of insight I perceived the real reason I had bought the pistol. I needed it for the execution of a monster.

Don't let me become one of them!

If only I could direct my hand to squeeze the trigger!

Lamia

Max Rohmer could not believe his ears. He was sitting in his plush air-conditioned office in Santa Monica. A dense black beard bristled his middle-aged face. As a psychiatrist he had treated hundreds of psychotics and neurotics over the years but never one like Eddie Copley. How did teenagers dream up these hallucinations? Rohmer wondered.

"Now, Eddie, tell me as calmly as possible what exactly happened," said Rohmer.

Eddie shifted his gangly body apprehensively on his leatherette easy chair. He scratched his reddish blond hair.

"They're gonna kill me, Doc."

"Relax. Nobody's going to kill you."

Eddie shook his head helplessly. "They're gonna kill me."

"Let's just back up. OK? I want to make sure I have the details straight in my mind."

"I already told you, Doc."

"Tell me again."

"Like I said, Two-UPS and me were cruising for chicks—"

"Two-UPS?"

"Mark Daniels. We call him Two-UPS because that's what's on his license plate."

"Go on."

"We weren't scoring with our cruising, so we got together some of the guys to go to a cathouse. We got Mickey McDougal, Guillermo, Nicky, and Toad. Two-UPS had to back out at the last minute. He had to babysit for his kid sister.

"We decided to go in Guillermo's car. He's a lowrider. His car goes up and down. You know, on hydraulic jacks. He's got them rigged to a spare battery in his convertible. Whenever he sees a chick he likes, he makes the Chevy go up and down. It looks weird. You'd have to see it.

"We parked on Sunset Boulevard a couple blocks from the cathouse. Guillermo didn't want anyone to see his car in front of the cathouse. That's why we parked down the street from it. Toad got cold feet when we walked up Sunset. He dawdled behind us with his hands in his pockets. He looks just like a toad, Doc. You ought to see him.

"'Are you chicken?' Nicky yelled at him.

"'No.'

"'Come on, then.'

"Toad caught up with us. He didn't look too happy about it. I think his father's a preacher or something. But Toad likes girls as much as the rest of us, so he came along.

"Have you ever seen the cathouse, Doc? It's huge. It looks like one of those phony Moorish mansions in a Hollywood movie. There are lots of weird statues around it. Gargoyles and dwarves. Some Arabian sheik owns the place, I think. He had those statues put in special.

"We walked up the long deserted driveway in the dark. If it wasn't for a piece of moon, we wouldn't've been able to see where we were going. There wasn't a single light on in that cathouse.

"'Are you sure anyone's home?' asked Toad.

"'They're in, all right,' said Mickey. 'They just don't want the cops to know.'

"'Let's go back,' said Toad. 'I don't think I can afford this.'

"'We know you got the money,' said Mickey. 'We saw it in your wallet. Remember?'

"Guillermo laughed. 'You can't avoid it, Toad. Today's the day you become a man.'

"'We're gonna have some fun tonight, ain't we, fellas?' said Nicky. 'I hear they got some incredible broads in this place.'

"We walked onto the front porch. The moon went behind a cloud. We couldn't see a thing.

"'Where's the doorbell?' asked Mickey.

"I felt alongside the door for it.

"'Let's leave,' said Toad nervously.

"'We just got here,' said Nicky. 'What are you talking about?'

"I found the doorbell. I pushed it. Nobody answered the door for a couple minutes. I pushed the bell again.

"'You see. Nobody's here,' said Toad. 'What did I tell you? Let's go play *Space Invaders*.'

"'Knock it off,' said Mickey. 'They're probably sizing us up from one of the windows to make sure we're not cops.'

"We waited a few more minutes. A tall gaunt man with greasy black hair and bloodshot black eyes opened the door. We could make him out because of the hall's lamplight. He wore a black trench coat.

"I didn't like the looks of him. Why was he wearing a trench coat inside the palace? Sometimes I see guys in black trench coats coming out of porno theaters. This guy reminded me of one of them. I don't trust them. This guy had that same fixed look in his eyes that they always have.

"'I'm Netzi,' he said. 'What can I do for you?'

"'A friend of ours told us about—you know, the good times you have here,' Mickey stammered.

"Mickey. He was the brave one of us. He was stammering.

"'I think I know what you mean,' said Netzi.

"I didn't like that weird glint in his hard black eyes. He had eyes like onyx. I was beginning to feel like Toad. I wanted to beat it. What was I doing at a cathouse, anyway? I loved Nancy. Of course she never paid the slightest bit of attention to me. She loved someone else. So I guess that's why I was there at the cathouse.

"I definitely didn't like Netzi, though. There was no way in the world I'd ever like this guy. I should've left, shouldn't I've, Doc? Chippies aren't any good for you. You can't ever have what you want in this world. You can't have nothing. You can't do nothing. If you can have it, it's probably evil. It doesn't make any sense to me, Doc, but that's what it seems like. Nancy doesn't even know I exist. She's the one I want, but she doesn't want me. That's the way it always is. Or vice versa.

"So there I was at the cathouse. I know I should've been studying or doing my homework, but I wanted to have a little fun once in a while, like everybody else."

"That's all part of growing up, Eddie," said Rohmer. "You may get what you want later on in life. Some people get what they want early in life. Others have to be patient and wait for their time to come."

"It's no fun waiting. How long do I have to wait?"

Maybe forever, thought Rohmer. "Everybody's different. I can't say."

"Well, I shouldn't've been at that cathouse. That's for sure.

"'Come in,' said Netzi.

"It wasn't like any of us bolted inside that palace or anything. We took our own sweet time about it. Mickey and Guillermo sort of eased on in first. Nicky's eyes got big, but he followed them. I hung back with Toad. Neither of us budged. The phony palace gave me the creeps.

"Then I scoped out this incredible blonde kind of gliding behind Netzi. She was the bomb! She had a thin pink negligee on. I thought I could see right through it. Her lips looked like a rose. My heart went crazy. My mouth watered. My eyes steamed up. I could hardly see.

"Netzi was about to close the door on me and Toad. I didn't want to lose my chance. I shot into the hallway. Toad tagged along on my heels because he was scared to be left alone outside.

"My eyes were bleary. Everything seemed dreamy. I wanted to ogle the blonde, but I was too shy. Instead I stared at the floor. A brunette came in. Her body was even better than the blonde's. I didn't look at it though. I liked it so much that I got nervous looking at it. You can understand that, can't you, Doc?"

Rohmer's mind wandered. He was thinking about something he had heard last week from one of his patients. *Society rejects me, so I reject it*, Rohmer recalled. Who had said that? That writer he was treating. That writer who had undergone therapy last Tuesday.

"Are you listening, Doc?" asked Eddie.

"Yes. Go ahead."

"The two chicks took us into a room upstairs. They told us to eyeball some photos and wait. They wanted us to pick the hooker we wanted. We gave the photos the once-over. Guess what happened? (They weren't photos of nudes. The chicks wore tight clothes, is all. I guess Netzi didn't want us to see any of the good stuff without paying for it in advance.) Well, guess what?"

"What?" asked Rohmer.

"We all picked the same chick, without even knowing it. We started arguing with each other. The funny thing is we only had a photo of her torso. The rest of the chicks, we could see their entire bodies.

"'I wish I could see her—' Toad stuttered.

"'Her what?' said Nicky.

"'Her—you know.'

"'Spit it out,' said Guillermo.

"'On the other pictures you can see everything, I mean,' said Toad. He blushed.

"'Her ass,' laughed Guillermo. 'That's what he's talking about. If you don't like her, pick someone else, Toad. We can't all go to her.'

"Toad shook his head.

"'She's still the best,' he mumbled.

"'Everybody can't have her,' said Mickey. 'What are we gonna do?'

"'I picked her first,' said Nicky, 'so I get her.'

"'That's only because you got to see her picture before the rest of us,' I said.

"'So what?'

"'We'll never get anywhere like this,' said Mickey. 'Let's draw lots.'

"Everybody nodded. What was fair was fair. Mickey had a book of matches. He tore out five matches. He tore them in different lengths. He held them in his hand in such a way that we couldn't see how long they were.

"'Go ahead and pick,' he said. 'The longest one goes first, and down the line like that.'

"We each picked a match from his hand. It figured that I ended up with the shortest match. That meant I had to go last. Needless to say, I felt like I was sucking hind tit—if you'll pardon my French, Doc. Mickey ended up with the match that was remaining in his hand after the rest of us had picked ours. It turned out to be the longest. He jumped about a foot in the air with joy.

"The blonde opened the door.

"'Have you chosen your partners?' she asked. She had an accent. I couldn't place it. Maybe it was Scandinavian.

"'We picked the same one,' said Mickey. 'Is that OK?'

"'That's fine,' she said emotionlessly.

"'We're gonna take turns. I get to go first.'

"She nodded at him. 'Come with me. Are you sure you can afford it?'

"Mickey scooped five crumpled twenty dollar bills from his trouser pocket. He unfolded them in front of her face. They were the dirtiest bills I had ever seen. They were wrinkled in a million places and torn in a few others. It looked as though he had bunched them in his hand for a couple hours and sweated on them. The blonde didn't seem to notice. All she cared about were the numbers on the corners.

"'Let's go,' she said.

"She hooked her arm around his and left. I guess that's why they call them hookers."

"As a matter of fact," said Rohmer, "the name derives from a General Hooker in the Civil War.

He used to allow hookers to follow his regiments when they marched."

"How about that? You learn something every day. But I like my explanation better. The blonde told us to wait our turns. Mickey left with her. He was grinning from ear to ear and leering at us as he split. We all envied him. Some guys have all the luck.

"I didn't like waiting. It made me antsy. Waiting for something to happen is always worse than the thing that eventually happens. Did you ever notice that?

"Nicky and Guillermo sat down near a coffee table in the center of the room. Toad and me paced around like fathers in a hospital waiting for their babies to be born. Toad settled down after a while and stared out the window. The window overlooked the backyard. It was still pretty dark outside, but stars had come out to help the moon give light. Toad motioned for me to come over to him.

"'It looks like a cemetery down there, doesn't it?' he said.

"He was right. A bunch of tombstones jutted from the flat ground beneath the window.

"'I didn't know we were next to a cemetery,' I said.

"'I don't think it's a public cemetery, or like that. I bet it's private. Netzi must own that land down there. It's right beside his palace.'

"'Pretty strange, if you ask me,' I said. 'I never saw a cemetery in someone's yard.'

"'Neither did I. Maybe we should get out of here.'

"Nicky heard us talking.

"'What a couple of scaredy-cats,' he said. 'A cemetery can't hurt you.' He looked out the window. 'What's the big deal about a cemetery? These rich guys can do anything they want. This Netzi wants his own cemetery, so he has someone install one for him. That's all there is to it.'

"'Maybe, but I don't like it,' said Toad. He scratched his Adam's apple. He looked worried.

"The blonde opened the door. It was Guillermo's turn. He happily went out with her.

"'Where's Mickey?' I asked.

"'He's waiting in the living room,' she answered.

"It went on like that until I was the only one left in the room.

"I kept looking at this big clock near the door. Everything was so quiet I could hear it ticking. It was one of those clocks that have a pendulum swinging in a glass case down below the face. I think they're called grandfather clocks. Anyway, this one had a pendulum with a brass ball the size of a grapefruit on the end of it. I couldn't sit down and relax. That clock kept ticking louder and louder. You couldn't believe how quiet it was except for that clock. The quiet was driving me just as crazy as that noisy clock. I kept focusing my mind on the ticking, so I wouldn't pay attention to the eerie silence. I heard footsteps . . .

"Finally it was my turn. I tore out of that room in a flash. I couldn't wait to get out of there. I wanted to get this over with and meet the other guys. The blonde walked beside me. She had blue eyes that looked vacant like fish eyes. I'm thinking shark's eyes, I don't know why. I guess that's what hooking does to you. It scared me. I didn't want to end up having eyes that looked like that. There was

26

this feeling of coldness about her that gave me the willies."

"It was probably her lack of feeling that conveyed this sense of coldness to you," said Rohmer. "Prostitutes are emotionally bankrupt because of the loveless lives they have to lead."

"I'll tell you the real reason she was cold in a minute. You said you wanted me to give you all the details first. As I was saying, this hooker took me to Lamia. That was the name of the chippie I was going to, according to my escort who was leading me down the hallway to Lamia's room.

"The floor had a velvety maroon carpet. The closed doors on our sides had gold crown molding around their edges. I heard a bestial sound from beyond the door on my right. The blonde must've noticed my ears pricking up at the noise.

"'That's one of your friends having fun,' she said. A leer twisted her pale lips.

"'I thought everybody decided to see Lamia,' I said, perplexed.

"'Some of them had extra money. They wanted to have more fun.'

"I paused near the door. I couldn't hear any more sounds. I wondered who it was. Toad? Who would've believed it? I heard moaning then nothing.

"'This way,' she said.

"We stopped in front of a door near the spiral staircase.

"'This is Lamia's room,' the blonde said.

"I couldn't understand why she hadn't asked me about the money.

"'What about the money?' I asked. 'Should I pay you now?'

"'You can pay Lamia.'

"The blonde hooker seemed to float away down the stairs.

"I stood alone in front of the door. I gripped the doorknob. My heart went crazy, thumping like a machine gun. My heart literally caught in my throat. I thought I would suffocate. I told myself to calm down. I was determined to have fun, and that was that. I cracked the door.

"As the door opened wider, I could make out Lamia lying on a round bed that had a pink silk counterpane. She lay between the pink sheets. Her fine honey hair tumbled down her rosy cheeks. Unlike the blonde hooker who had escorted me here, Lamia looked full of life. Maybe that was why everyone in our group was drawn to her— because she looked so healthy. She had full, pouty, bright red lips. She wore a bra. No other clothing that I could see. Her round white shoulders lay against the fluffy pink pillow behind her back. Silk lace fringed the pillowcase. She smiled at me. She winked.

"I approached her. I trembled with excitement. Her chest heaved with desire. She craned her neck toward me. The sheets slipped away from her naked waist. I froze in shock.

"It was filthy. It was disgusting. Doc, you can't believe what I saw."

"I've been with a woman, Eddie. I'm not a priest."

Revulsion swept over Eddie. He held his hands over his face to shut out his hair-raising memory of Lamia.

"I don't want to remember it," he said. "I don't want to remember."

"There's nothing to be frightened of. If you talk about it, you'll feel better. Believe me. Being with a woman is part of growing up. It's nothing to be ashamed of. Sex is a normal urge. Don't let yourself be disgusted by it."

"But, Doc, it was slimy. It was green. And silver. I saw it all when she slithered out of the sheets. I wanted to puke."

"I can't understand your unnatural disgust for sex," said Rohmer. "Is there something in your past that I should know about? Were you molested as a child?"

"Doc, for crying out loud, listen to me! Will you listen to me!"

"That's why I'm here."

"From the waist down she was a snake. I swear to you. She grabbed my shoulders. She drew my face toward hers. She opened her mouth. Fangs as big as tiger teeth drooled behind her lips. She lunged for my throat. She hissed. She writhed. I was so shocked and disgusted I couldn't budge.

"A grisly cry from the room next door distracted her. She paused. I seized my chance. I pulled away from her. She hissed. She spat in rage. I ran for my life out the door.

"I flew down the stairs. When I got to the living room I looked inside for the other guys. No Mickey. No Guillermo. No Nicky. No Toad. I glanced back up the stairs. I didn't see Lamia following me. I didn't know what to do. I didn't want to run into her again, but I wanted to find the guys. I ran back up the stairs. I had to find them.

"I pressed my ear against the door beside Lamia's room. I heard a dripping sound.

"I burst into the room. Mickey and Guillermo were inside. Guillermo lay on his back on the floor. Two hookers knelt over him. They were sinking their fangs into his throat. Blood soaked the fronts of their negligees. Mickey lay on his back on the bed. His head lolled over the edge. Blood dripped onto the floor from his torn jugular. *Drip, drip, drip*. The brunette hooker chewed and sucked his shredded throat.

"One of the hookers on Guillermo crawled toward Mickey's neck. She rolled over onto her back. Then she slid on her back under Mickey's neck to catch Mickey's blood droplets in her mouth. Mickey and Guillermo looked dead to me. The chippies glanced up at me, but they didn't care. They were getting too turned on glutting themselves on fresh blood.

"I raced down the hall into the room where I earlier had heard that bestial groan. I flung open the door. Nicky was sprawled motionlessly on his face on the floor, his neck at an impossible angle. Toad sat on a rocking chair that creaked back and forth. His contorted black and blue neck must've been broken. His eyes stared dead at the ceiling. From where I stood I couldn't tell whether the chippies had gnawed his throat yet. I didn't stick around to find out. Nicky and Toad were past help. I ran like hell.

"I collided with Netzi in the hallway. It was like running into a steel pole. I fell sideways against the wall. He just stood there, unaffected by our collision. He glared at me with his red eyes. I regained my balance and sped down the stairway.

"Well, you can see, Doc, I made it. Here I am. It was so dark outside, nobody could spot me when I fled."

"Are you telling me the prostitutes murdered your friends last night?"

"They weren't prostitutes. They were vampires! That's what I've been trying to tell you.

30

They're gonna kill me next because I know about them."

Eddie leapt to his feet. Wringing his hands he paced the office.

"Why couldn't the police locate the corpses?" asked Rohmer.

"How should I know? Maybe Netzi buried them. You and I both know their parents have no idea where their kids are. Their parents will never see them again. That's a fact. We've got to kill those vampires. We can't let them get away with what they did."

"Did the police interrogate the hookers?"

"No. They searched Netzi's house. They couldn't find a soul. Of course not. The cops went to his house during the daytime. Vampires sleep during the day. The cops told me I'm nuts. They told my parents I need professional help."

"Which is why you're here with me, Eddie. And I can help you as long as you're honest with me."

Eddie ignored him. "They didn't believe a word I told them. But believe me, Doc, I know what I saw."

"Do you honestly believe you saw a woman that was half snake?" Rohmer narrowed his eyes thoughtfully. He adjusted his black-framed glasses on his nose.

"That's right," said Eddie. "Lamia."

"Listen to yourself, Eddie. Do you really believe what you're saying?"

"Come with me to the cathouse tonight. I'll show you. I'm not crazy. I don't belong in the loony bin."

Eddie must be delirious, thought Rohmer. Yet Eddie didn't appear disoriented. He seemed in full control of his faculties. He genuinely believed he saw vampires. Something must have happened at Netzi's house last night. But what? Something so bad that it had traumatized Eddie and caused him to dream up this wild hallucination to explain away the shock to his system.

"Are you with me, Doc?"

"Do you realize what you're telling me, Eddie?"

"I know it sounds crazy. What have you got to lose by going with me to Netzi's tonight?"

Rohmer shrugged. "All right."

"Good. We'll have to take crosses and wooden stakes to protect ourselves."

"Eddie," said Rohmer in a patronizing tone.

"We've got to destroy them before they kill more people."

Eddie retreated toward the door.

"I'll pick you up at your house at eight o'clock," said Rohmer.

"We've got to crush the evil before it spreads," said Eddie. His voice trembled.

He left the office.

First we must decide if the evil exists, thought Rohmer. *Society rejects me, so I reject society. Then why should I do anything for anyone? Why should I concern myself with evil? But society doesn't reject me. I'm paid well. I make a decent living. I have no complaints. That writer I'm treating is the one who can't find a job. I can understand his complaints. I can understand why he rejects society. Life is rough when you can't get a job. I don't have that problem. Why are you thinking, Rohmer? Reason has nothing to do with life. If evil exists in Netzi's mansion, I must deal with it.*

Azalea leaves shuffled overhead in the cool night. Rohmer and Eddie stole up to the front door of Netzi's mansion. A ragged grey cloud lay hooked on a horn of the nail clipping of fluorescent moon in the gloomy sky.

"The palace is dark. Just like last night," said Eddie.

He handed Rohmer a wooden cross.

Rohmer shook his head.

"Come on, Doc. It's our only protection."

"No."

"Why not? It won't hurt you."

"I feel like an idiot carrying that thing around."

"Take it for my sake. It'll make me feel better."

Rohmer shrugged. Grudgingly, he accepted the cross. He inserted it into his trouser back pocket. He forgot about it.

"Ring the doorbell," he said.

"I'm glad you parked in the driveway. If things get hot, we can scram fast."

Eddie carried a navy blue Hollywood Park polyester satchel in his left hand.

"What do you have in there?" asked Rohmer.

"Wooden stakes and two hammers."

Rohmer closed his eyes and shook his head in disbelief.

Eddie contemplated the doorbell. "I think we should break in."

"It's illegal. Netzi could have us thrown in jail."

"If he answers the door, he'll recognize me. He'll be ready for us. We won't have a chance. Let's go in through the window."

They padded across the moist slippery front lawn to the side of the palace.

"We shouldn't be doing this, Eddie. You didn't say anything about breaking in."

"We've got to catch them off guard."

Eddie and Rohmer edged toward a window.

"I was curious about the name Lamia," said Rohmer. "I looked it up last night in an encyclopedia. I had never heard of the name before you mentioned it. It's the name of a monster from Greek mythology. The top half is a woman. The bottom half is a serpent."

"What did I tell you? Now do you believe me?"

"It lures children in order to suck their blood, according to Greek myth."

"I told you I wasn't crazy."

"You probably read about the lamia somewhere and got it mixed up with what happened here last night."

Eddie grimaced. "You still don't believe me."

He withdrew a hammer from the satchel. He thrust the head of the hammer through the window's screen. As he pulled it out, the hammer's claws ripped a wide hole in the screen. He inserted the hammer into his waistband. He reached through the hole with both hands. He grabbed the opposite borders of the hole in the screen and widened the hole, ripping the screen. From the waist up he leaned through the hole. He lifted the window.

"There," he said. "We can fit through that."

"We shouldn't be doing this," said Rohmer.

"We should've brought Two-UPS. I don't know how many of them live here. There are at least three. I hope we can handle them by ourselves."

Eddie picked up his satchel and crawled through the hole.

"If what you say is true that they're vampires," said Rohmer, feeling like a fool even as he spoke, "we should have come here during the day when they're in their coffins."

"Somebody would see us break into his house during the daytime. They'd call the cops. We have to break in at night. We don't have any choice."

"Let's talk to these people before we start pounding stakes through their hearts. Maybe we can find out what's really going on here."

"You can't talk to these people. They're not people. They're vampires."

Eddie and Rohmer were standing in the darkened dining room. They skulked toward the hallway, which was steeped in shadows. A moldy odor hung in the air. The overwhelming silence bore an aura of finality about it. It was preternaturally quiet. Something had to give. Eddie clenched his cross.

"Let's go to Lamia's room," he whispered. "She seems to have some sort of control over the others."

They crept up the spiral staircase. The treads creaked under their weight, sounding as loud as screams of terror in the still house. Eddie winced each time he heard the creaking. He feared lest the noise would alert the vampires to his and Rohmer's presence.

Eddie unzipped his satchel in preparation for the assault. He would now be able to dig out the stakes and hammers as rapidly as possible when the time came for their use. He and Rohmer neared Lamia's door.

"Be careful," murmured Rohmer. "If the owners are here, they could shoot us as intruders. No jury in the world would convict them either."

Eddie eased open the door to Lamia's room. It squeaked on its hinges.

Somebody flicked on the light switch. Light flooded the room. Eddie saw Lamia writhing in her bed. Her bloodshot blue eyes flared at the sight of him and Rohmer. She was wide awake. Saliva dribbled out the corners of her rosy mouth. Snarls rose like barbs from her throat. Seething with anger she bared her fangs. She thrust her breasts out at them as she reared up in her bed.

Eddie held up his cross. It had no effect. Lamia didn't even wince. Astonishment and horror swept over Eddie's face.

"I don't understand," he said.

He fumbled for the hammers and stakes in the satchel.

"Let's not do anything rash," said Rohmer.

"What are you talking about? We got to destroy her."

"How do we know she's evil?"

"I told you what she did last night," said Eddied, flabbergasted. "She killed my friends. If that isn't evil, what is?"

Can I believe him? thought Rohmer. "I don't know."

"Look at her fangs! She's a monster."

"She has bad teeth. That doesn't mean she killed anyone. Where are the corpses?"

"The vampires obviously hid them somewhere. The cops already searched the place and couldn't find a thing. I know that. I also know what I saw. I saw these vampires kill my friends. You can see for yourself she isn't human."

"She looks human to me."

"If you pulled that sheet down that's covering her, you'd see she's part snake."

Lamia's pink and white vibrant female flesh glowed above the pink sheet that she was clutching to her stomach.

"If she's a vampire, why doesn't your cross affect her?" asked Rohmer.

"I don't know," said Eddie, baffled. "I don't get it."

"Do we have the right to kill her?"

"She murdered my friends," Eddie pleaded.

"If we kill her, we'll be stooping to her bestial level."

"What do you want to do? Bust her? Put a vampire on trial?"

"Let's think about this before we start killing people."

"If we don't kill her, she'll go right on killing."

Rohmer scratched his head in thought. "What if we lock her up somewhere? Then she can't do anyone any harm."

The hallway floor creaked. Eddie spun around.

Netzi was standing behind him and Rohmer. Netzi's black eyes flashed red like burning coals.

Eddie shoved his cross at Netzi's face. Netzi drew back. He cowered in the hall.

"You see, Doc, he's a vampire," said Eddie.

Lamia writhed off the bed toward Eddie and Rohmer. Rohmer could now see her green and blue scales glinting in the lamplight. The scales started at her waist. Instead of two legs she had a snakelike tail, as Eddie had informed him earlier. Rohmer recoiled in disgust.

"We've got to kill them, or they'll kill us," said Eddie.

"Is there no other way?" asked Rohmer.

"None. Netzi's afraid of the cross. Let's get him first. Grab a hammer and stake!"

Reluctantly, Rohmer nodded. He seized a hammer and a wooden stake from Eddie's satchel.

With Eddie he charged Netzi in the hall.

"Through the heart!" Eddie yelled.

Netzi scrambled down the stairs in his haste to flee. Eddie and Rohmer chased him. A brunette and a blonde vampire confronted Eddie and Rohmer on the stair's landing, impeding their pursuit of Netzi. The two vampires hissed. They seemed to glide across the floor. They scowled as they advanced toward Eddie and Rohmer.

Eddie jammed a stake into the brunette's heart. She let out a bloodcurdling shriek. Her blood spurted onto Eddie's hands and throat. Some of it squirted into his mouth. Screwing up his face he spat the blood out. The brunette reeled. She clutched the stake buried in her heart. She struggled to remove the stake. She could not extricate it. She stumbled backwards down the staircase. She tumbled down the steps, coming to a halt in a crumpled heap on the next floor's landing.

Rohmer wrestled with the blonde. Her fangs sought his throat. Eddie smashed the back of her skull with his hammer. Blood and bone shards gushed down her nape. She looked stunned. However, she continued to claw at Rohmer, seeking out his jugular with her saliva-dripping fangs.

Eddie darted into Lamia's bedroom. He snagged the satchel from the floor. He grasped a stake. He bolted back to the hallway. He plunged the stake into the blonde's back where he thought her heart was located. He hammered the stake into her. The stake splintered under the blows. The stake's point pierced her heart. Her strident scream rent the air. Her trembling left hand reached behind her back to grab the stake. She fell dead to the carpet before she could lay a hand on the stake.

Rohmer stared in horror at her.

Lamia wriggled toward them.

Rohmer jerked the cross from his back pocket.

"It won't work," said Eddie, watching Rohmer. "I already tried."

Rohmer thrust the cross into her face. In repulsion she covered her face with the backs of her hands.

Eddie's face registered confusion. "Why does she fear your cross but not mine?"

"Because I'm an atheist."

Eddie shook his head in bewilderment.

Three vampires charged down the corridor at them.

"There are too many of them!" cried Eddie. "Let's get out of here."

Rohmer and Eddie skedaddled down the stairs. The duo barged through the front door. They fled toward their car in the driveway. They piled into the blue Toyota sedan.

Rohmer started the car. He put the car in gear. He sped away from the mansion into the street. A car pursued them.

"You got to lose them," said Eddie.

"What does it look like I'm doing? Barbecuing hot dogs?"

Eddie gave him a look. After a while Eddie said, "I'm not kidding. Why did Lamia fear your cross but not mine?"

"I've been thinking about that," answered Rohmer, his hands on the steering wheel. "I might have the answer."

"What is it?"

"Remember, the lamia is a monster from Greek mythology."

"What's your point?"

"How did you hold your cross when you confronted her with it?"

Eddie demonstrated by holding his cross in front of him.

"Is that exactly how you held it?" asked Rohmer.

"Yeah."

"Give me the cross."

Eddie handed the cross to him. His left hand on the steering wheel, Rohmer clutched the cross with his right.

"This is how I held it," said Rohmer.

Eddie shook his head in confusion. "Big deal. So?"

"You held the cross at the bottom, forming a Latin cross. I held it in the middle, forming a Greek cross."

"I'm lost, Doc. What are you trying to say? What's all this about Greek crosses and Latin crosses?"

"A Greek cross has four sides of equal lengths. Since the lamia is a product of Greek mythology, she only responds to a Greek cross."

"If you say so," deadpanned Eddie, not buying into Rohmer's explanation. "What's the matter?"

Rohmer's Toyota wheezed and jerked to a halt. Rohmer squinted at the speedometer.

"We're running on fumes," he said.

Rohmer glanced in the rearview mirror. He saw the car chasing them close the gap between them. Eddie turned around to peer out the Toyota's rear window. His eyes bulged wide at the sight of the car that was speeding toward them, its headlights' beams on high. He seized a hammer and a stake that lay on the backseat. Rohmer snatched his weapons on the front seat.

"Out of here!" cried Eddie.

Hammers and stakes in their hands, Rohmer and Eddie clambered out of the Toyota onto San Vicente Boulevard. They ran to a blue plywood hoarding that surrounded an excavation site for a new building. The sedan full of vampires pulled up beside them.

"If they morph into bats, we're fucked," Eddie told Rohmer.

"In here," said Rohmer.

They ducked into an opening in the hoarding. They hustled down the temporary stairs to the dirt bottom of the excavation pit. They anxiously surveyed the pit.

A network of rebar about a foot off the ground connected to concrete columns covered the dirt floor of the pit. Four walls of dirt crested with plywood boards encompassed Eddie and Rohmer. They saw no way out.

"Watch your step," said Rohmer, surveying the rebar crosshatching the ground.

"We're trapped," said Eddie.

"Our only hope is that they didn't see us duck into here," said Rohmer.

Eddie gazed upward behind them. He pulled a face. "Then it's hopeless."

At the head of the stairs stood the vampires. They were congregating behind Netzi. They looked straight at Eddie and Rohmer. Netzi descended the jerrybuilt wooden staircase. Knowing vampire lore Eddie was not surprised to see that Netzi, like any self-respecting male vampire, was wearing a black cape over his shoulders with a purple silk lining. Three vampires followed Netzi down. Lamia brought up the rear. She squirmed deftly down the wooden planks on her slimy scales.

"Know any prayers, Doc?" asked Eddie in a quaking voice, watching the vampires circle them.

"I told you I'm an atheist," answered Rohmer.

Eddie gaped at Rohmer. "Still?" Eddie looked back toward the vampires.

"Let's keep our backs toward each other to protect our rears," said Rohmer.

Eddie agreed. He and Rohmer both clutched wooden stakes and hammers as they shifted into position to ward off the vampires. Eddie had three more wooden stakes wedged between his leather belt and his jeans.

The vampires kept circling. The circle tightened by degrees, hemming Rohmer and Eddie in. The vampires charged.

Rohmer and Eddie furiously thrust and jabbed their stakes into the creatures' dead flesh.

"Aim for their hearts!" cried Eddie.

Blood spattered Rohmer and Eddie. Fangs slashed at their arms. Rohmer and Eddie fought back with the stakes in their hands. Rohmer stabbed one of the vampires through the heart.

"I need another stake!" he called to Eddie.

Eddie plucked a stake from his belt. He offered the stake to Rohmer. Rohmer grasped it. In short order he began thrusting it at a vampire that was closing in on his neck.

Lamia tried to slither up Eddie's leg. He kept kicking her in the face to stave her off.

Rohmer yanked his cross from his trousers' back pocket. He flung it on the dirt in front of him. Netzi cringed and backed away from the cross.

Rohmer plunged a stake into a female vampire's heart. She wailed. Blood gurgled from her gaping mouth. She collapsed on the ground. Aghast, Rohmer watched her body crumble into ashes. The two other vampires that lay on the dirt with stakes in their hearts began disintegrating as well. Dust clouds mushroomed from the moldering ashes of their corpses. A sickening odor permeated the air.

When he smelled the putrid stench, Eddie choked back vomit that rose in his throat. He and Rohmer had wasted three of the vampires. That left Netzi and Lamia.

Vampire blood and cuts from vampire claws streaked Eddie and Rohmer. The duo's clothes hung in shreds on their throbbing bodies. Eddie sighed with relief that neither of them had been bitten by the vampires' deadly venomous fangs.

Netzi snagged the wooden handle of a steel shovel that lay on the dirt. He swung the shovel at Rohmer. It caught the side of Rohmer's head. Rohmer tumbled to the dirt. Netzi tossed the shovel down, leering in triumph.

Eddie drove a stake into Lamia's heart. Her dying screams reverberated through the night. Blood jetted into his eyes and mouth. Lamia's frozen blue eyes stared vacantly at the moon. Eddie did not have time to wipe his face off. He fixed his attention on Netzi.

Eddie charged Netzi. Tangling his feet in the rebar in front of him, Eddie tripped. He toppled to the ground. He winced in pain as he banged his knees against the ridged steel rebar.

Netzi lunged at Rohmer's prostrate body. Baring his fangs Netzi knelt down and collared Rohmer's neck in his icy hands. Netzi squeezed Rohmer's jugular in his hands. The vein distended and throbbed under the pressure. Lusting for blood Netzi jacked open his mouth. He prepared to take a bite out of the pulsating jugular.

Eddie jumped to his feet, ignoring the pain in his knees as he landed upright. Eddie wheeled on Netzi. He kicked Netzi's face. Netzi rolled off Rohmer onto his back. Eddie leapt onto Netzi's supine body. Netzi unleashed his fangs. He growled at Eddie. Netzi's bloodshot eyes became a lurid red. They burned like hot embers in Netzi's face.

Eddie had to look away from the intensity of Netzi's fiery gaze, but not before he had aimed a stake at Netzi's heart and rammed it home. Netzi bucked and flung Eddie off his chest. Netzi jumped to his feet. He grabbed the stake that protruded from his rib cage. He staggered a few steps. Gloating, he yanked the bloody stake out of his chest. A mist of blood from his chest sprayed the air. He hurled the stake to the ground.

Eddie stood nonplussed. He could not believe his eyes. Netzi the vampire should be dead. What the hell had happened? Eddie wondered.

"You missed his heart," Rohmer moaned as he lay on the ground.

Netzi grinned sadistically at Eddie, raising his arms and spreading his cape at his sides.

Eddie reached for another stake in his belt. He clutched air. Stunned, he gazed down at his belt. He had no stakes left. He thought he had one left. It must have fallen out during the fracas. He clapped eyes on a hammer lying in the dirt. Careful not to trip on any rebar, he lunged for the hammer.

As he brought the hammer up, he swung it at Netzi's face. The case-hardened steel hammerhead obliterated Netzi's nose. Netzi evinced no pain. He

44

shoved Eddie away from him. Eddie was no match for Netzi's supernatural strength.

Rohmer tackled Netzi from behind. Netzi fell flat on his face. Eddie buried the claws of the hammer into Netzi's back. Blood oozed from Netzi's back where the claws had struck him. The hammer remained embedded between Netzi's ribs. Netzi reached behind his back. He wrenched the hammer out of his cold flesh. Cold red blood sluiced over his hand. Hammer in hand, he stood up. He heaved the hammer at Eddie's head. Eddie ducked.

The hammer must not have gone deep enough, Eddie decided with undisguised horror.

Netzi flew at him in a rage. Eddie beat it. He stumbled over a crowbar that the construction workers at the pit had left behind. Eddie stopped. He groped for the crowbar at his feet. He snagged it. He saw Netzi charging toward him. Eddie swung the crowbar at Netzi's neck. The steel claws of the crowbar slammed into Netzi's throat. Inexorably, Netzi kept on coming. A deep gash in his neck vomited blood.

Rohmer chased Netzi from behind. Rohmer shattered Netzi's spine with a two-handed blow from his hammer. Rohmer heard the muffled crack of bones in Netzi's spinal column. Netzi whirled around. He confronted Rohmer. With one hand he grabbed Rohmer's throat and began heaving Rohmer off the ground.

Eddie discovered a toolbox on the dirt near the area where the crowbar had lain. He removed a cold chisel from the toolbox. He thrust the cold chisel into Netzi's upper back. Netzi groaned. He slackened his grasp on Rohmer's throat. Gasping for breath Rohmer dropped to his knees. Netzi reached behind his back to yank out the chisel.

But Eddie's aim had been true. The chisel had burst Netzi's heart.

Netzi toppled to the ground. He let loose an agonizing scream. He fell on his back. The impetus of his fall drove the cold chisel deeper into his heart. Netzi's bloodred eyes popped from his head. His body commenced to disintegrate before Eddie's eyes. The body crackled into dust, discharging a rancid stench.

Eddie reeled back from the overpowering stink of decayed flesh.

"Now *we* are murderers," Rohmer managed to utter through his sore throat. He massaged the reddened welts on his neck.

"What else could we do?" said Eddie. "It was them or us. Look at it this way. We were executioners."

"Does it make any difference how you say it? Murder is murder."

"Doc, how can you murder a vampire? They're already dead in the first place. And look." He gestured with his hands at Netzi's ashes on the ground. "There's no corpus delicious."

"Corpus delicti," Rohmer corrected him.

Eddie cast around the dirt pit. The only trace left by the vampires was their dust. "Whatever. If there's no bodies, there's no murders. Any way you wanna look at it, the monsters are gone now."

"Evil never goes away. It only changes shape. It will be here as long as man."

"All right, you two," said the tense unshaven man on the stairs. "Toss your wallets over here." The disheveled, longhaired youth trained a revolver on them.

It's for You

At sixteen years of age Abby did not know if she was pretty, but people said she was. She had eyes like pools of blue sunlight, her mother once told her. She had a good figure. Most of the boys at high school were dying to date her. She lived in Van Nuys with two cats, her mother, who was a nurse, and her father, a prosperous, well-respected dentist.

She was sitting now in front of her desk mirror in her bedroom after dinner. The mirror had golf ball–sized lightbulbs surrounding it. Chewing grape bubblegum, she combed her long blond hair, wondering which boy to go out with this weekend.

The phone rang.

She answered it, pink comb in hand. "Hello."

"It's me," said the adenoidal voice, punctuated with heavy breathing.

"Who?"

"I watch you every day in your tight jeans . . . tight blouse . . . love it to death when you don't wear a bra—"

"Who is this?" Abby asked apprehensively. She squirmed in her chair.

"I know you want me . . . want *youuu*."

"Stop it! Who is this?"

"I love your body. What does it look like? . . . naked now? . . . every curve."

"Stop it! You're not funny. Who is this?"

"One night . . . your room . . . we'll do it—"

Terrified, Abby slammed the receiver into its cradle. She clenched her teeth. Eyes gaping, she stared at the phone. She dreaded it would ring again. She stayed motionless. She started jumping at the slightest sound: a car honking, a dog barking, the garbage disposal running downstairs in the kitchen.

The phone rang.

She jumped a foot off her chair. Stiff with fright, she backed away from the phone. It rang four times.

"Abby?" cried her father from the hallway. "Somebody on the phone for you."

"No!" she shouted through her closed door.

"What?"

"No."

"What do you mean—no?"

"Who is it?"

The silence dragged for a minute that seemed to last an hour to Abby.

"It's Phil," answered her father.

Abby sighed with relief. She picked up the handset. "Phil?"

"Hi, Abby."

"That wasn't funny." She recognized his voice, not that hideous nasal one.

"What wasn't funny?"

"Calling me up before and trying to scare me. Did you just watch *Scream* on TV or something?"

"Are you stoned? I don't know what you're talking about."

"Didn't you call me a few minutes ago?"

"No."

"You better not be lying."

"Do you want to go to a movie Friday night?"

"I don't know."

The lights on, lying in bed in her jeans she wondered who could have made the obscene phone call. Somebody at school? She did not recognize the voice. Some ugly guy probably playing a sick joke on her. The ugly ones were sickies because girls did not like them. That must be it. But who? She would never get him to stop until she found out his identity.

Was it George? She wondered. She had turned him down once. Always picking his nose. She could not stand his repulsive face. All he ever wanted to do was play video games. How could he stoop to something as sick as this?

The phone rang twice. She sat bolt upright. She hesitated before answering it. She eyed it suspiciously. She decided to answer it.

"Hello?" she said.

She heard heavy breathing.

"Stop it!" she cried. "Who is this?"

"I have a knife . . . better do as I say when I come," said the adenoidal voice.

"Go away! Leave me alone!"

". . . want you more than anybody I've ever wanted."

"Who are you?"

"My body, your body . . . touching."

"Who is this?"

"You know me, but . . ."

"But what?"

"But we can't do it. We're two islands a million miles apart, yet so near I can breathe on you."

"You're insane!"

"You want me as much as I want you. Admit it."

"I don't even know you."

"Yes, you do."

"I'm going to call the cops if you keep phoning me."

"What can they do?"

"They'll arrest you."

He laughed.

"I'm not kidding," she said.

"You won't press charges."

"I will."

"Not against me." He breathed heavily for several moments. "I can't wait to feel your naked body in my arms . . . ohhhh."

"Shut up!"

". . . wanted you for so long."

"Phil, is that you?"

"You don't know how hard it is for me to keep my hands off you."

". . . sick."

"Remember . . . knife."

She thought frantically about what she could do to make him stop. What if she tricked him? What if she pretended she wanted him to come to her? She had read somewhere that encouragement turned a rapist off.

"Do you want me to wear my hot pants?" she asked.

"Yes."

"I have a pair of purple satin ones."

"I've seen you in them. The tight ones?"

"And how about my boots with the spiked heels?"

"Yes, those too."

"Lipstick?"

"Yes."

"What kind? Red or lavender?"

"Bright red . . . kind you wear some nights."

"When I go to Hollywood?"

"When you go on your dates."

"I turn tricks in Hollywood on the weekends."

"What?"

"I'm new at it. I've only done it twice."

"You're lying!"

"No. Why should I?"

"Lying whore!"

"I'll do it with anyone if the price is right."

"You—"

"Except you."

"Me?"

"How much do you have?"

"Whore!"

"Didn't you know?"

"For money?"

"How much?"

". . . dirty little—"

"I thought you knew everything about me."

"Slut!"

"If you wanted to be one of my johns you should have called sooner."

Looking in her mirror she realized she was beginning to act the part: opening her mouth wide while chewing her gum, hand on her hip, head back. Carried away, the receiver pressed to her ear, she stood up and thrust her hip out, trying to look pert.

She felt oddly uninhibited talking to a complete stranger on the phone. She wanted to tell him things she would not tell her own mother, tell him about the time Phil slid his hand up her dress.

"Liar!" he said.

"Why should I lie? In Hollywood they call me Wet Lips." She posed for the mirror, licking her lips.

"You're a good girl . . . come from a nice home. I know."

"You think that's the real me?"

"I know it."

She giggled. "How naïve can you get?"

"You're just trying to sound mature."

"A lot you know."

"You're going to love it when I cut your hot pants off."

"You don't need a knife, only money."

He hung up.

Had it worked? she wondered. Had she gotten rid of him? She wished she could slow down her heartbeat. She paced around the room nervously, chewing her lower lip.

Who could it be? She wondered. He had said they were near each other. Could it be some boy she sat next to in one of her classes? She trembled. But he sounded older. It was hard to tell his age because of his nasal voice.

A teacher? A janitor? How could she possibly find out?

Frustrated, she struck her head above the ear with the heel of her hand. She had to figure out who this nutbag was before it was too late. Why did the psycho have to pick her of all girls? she wondered. Had she insulted one of her teachers and now it was payback time?

She shook her head in bewilderment. Her algebra teacher was ugly with a big nose and hairy warts on his face. Was he the one? she wondered. She had caught him staring at her in his class a couple of times.

But the caller knew about her hot pants. She had never worn them to school. It must be someone she had met at a party or disco. Or maybe the caller was lying, it suddenly occurred to her.

She switched off the light. She flung herself on her bed. She was giving herself a headache. She had to stop thinking about it.

She lay on her stomach, her face in her pillow. She moaned with pleasure as she felt the softness of her pillow against her cheek. She fluffed her pillow.

She heard the phone ring. *Oh no!* she thought. Her heart skipped a beat. She pounded her pillow with her fists.

Should she answer the phone or let it ring? she wondered. Glancing at the luminous face of the clock-radio on her desk, she saw it was eleven o'clock. The phone's ringing might wake Mom and Dad.

She decided she had better answer it, just so it would stop ringing. She lifted the handset. She slowly pulled it toward her. She strained to hear the voice, even as she prayed it wasn't the nutcase.

"Hello," she said meekly.

". . . you're alone now. I'll be there in a minute," said the adenoidal voice.

"No!"

"In a minute."

"I'm not alone," she blurted, tears streaking her cheeks.

"You are. I know."

"How can you know?"

Her bedroom door opened. A shaft of light from the corridor's lamp percolated into her dark room, framing a figure in the doorway. A phone in his left hand, the receiver in his right, he stood motionless. A swimmer's flesh-colored plastic nose plug pinched his nose. He set the hall phone on the carpet outside her door.

Throat tight, she watched him in terror. He reached behind his back. When his hand moved forward it had a butcher's knife in it. He held the haft of the knife in front of him. As he twisted the knife back and forth, she watched its blade catch the light.

"Don't yell, Abby, or I'll have to use this," he said in the adenoidal voice that sent shivers down her spine. "Take off your clothes."

Paralyzed with fright, her stomach sinking, she watched her father enter her room and shut the door behind him.

The Green Parrot

Why did my head always ache? What was the problem? I needed something to cheer me up.

On the spur of the moment, I bought a beautiful macaw. Its fluorescent green feathers were a joy to behold. It cheered me up just looking at its radiant feathers. The owner of the pet shop where I bought it said that he had imported it from Paraguay.

I'm getting ahead of myself. Probably on account of my aching head. Let me begin at the beginning . . . but why does it ache so damn much? Why can't I remember things? . . . Listen . . .

The day I bought the macaw I had lost a costly lawsuit and was feeling depressed. A colleague offered me Bolivian Marching Powder at the Century City law firm of Houser & Kidd where I worked. We did lines in the head and I felt on top of the world.

He sold me an ounce and I drove to the Sports Club LA, a hangar-sized brick red ceramic-tiled exclusive health club on Sepulveda in west LA. One of the white-uniformed Hispanic valets parked my Jag. I worked out for half an hour in the gym, trying to take my mind off my lousy day at work, not thinking about anything—just flexing my muscles, getting my circulation going.

Then I drove my burgundy Jag XJS to my condo in Brentwood, disengaging my cellular phone so nobody at the office would bug me. On the way home, I spotted the macaw in a pet-shop window.

I bought the macaw. I took it to my condo.

As I walked into the living room, I told the macaw, "Have a nice day, parrot."

"Have a nice day, parrot," the parrot replied.

I was surprised, for the pet-shop owner had neglected to tell me that the macaw could talk. It was a pleasant surprise, I had to admit. The parrot took my mind off my botched trial.

Wait. Let me get this straight. The parrot said, "Have a nice day, Parrot."

After I set the parrot's cage and its six-foot-high stand in a corner of the living room, I sat down on the futon. I used a razor to cut four lines on the glass-topped coffee table. I inhaled the blow through a red-and-white striped plastic straw.

The parrot seemed fascinated by my actions as it watched me. Or was it my imagination that it was watching me? It is difficult to tell where a parrot is looking, as its eyes are located on either side of its head. In any case, the very presence of the brightly colored parrot lifted my spirits.

I felt elated. I phoned Mandy to come over.

When I let her in she caught sight of the parrot on the spot. Delighted, she lilted over to its cage.

She was a CPA at MGM-Pathe Communications who dressed sharp. Her mauve minidress revealed her shapely white legs and, thanks to its tightness, outlined to a T the firm curve of her buttocks. Her high cheekbones and liquid cornflower blue eyes were the envy of her model and actress friends.

"He's gorgeous," she said, ogling the parrot. "What's his name?"

"Papagayo," I said.

"Papa who?"

"Papagayo. His full name is Papagayo Verde. It's Spanish for *Green Parrot*."

"How cute. Do you mind if I call him Papa?"

"Go ahead."

For some reason that I could not explain I was put out that she was paying more attention to the bird than she was to me. She could not get enough of Papa and even fed it some dried insect food I had bought for it at the pet store.

"Good Papa," she cooed as she fed it something that looked like a dehydrated cockroach.

Papa gobbled the insect. "Have a nice day, parrot."

Mandy laughed with joy on hearing it talk.

"I lost a big case today," I told her.

"That's too bad," she said, absorbed with feeding insect remains to the parrot.

I bridled at the tone of her voice. She sounded like she could care less. Hell, my career was on the line and all she cared about was that stupid parrot.

She fell to cawing at Papagayo. It cawed back at her. After all, it did not know it wasn't a crow. She found the macaw amusing. I was beginning to find it annoying.

She glanced at her diamond-encrusted Cartier watch. "Whoops! I'll be late to my hairdresser. Gotta run."

I followed her to the door. Once there, I clutched her fleshy upper arm. I smiled.

"I thought you were going to stay for a while," I said.

"I can't now."

She gently extricated her arm, smiled back at me, and peeled off.

I shut the door. I headed for the window. I insinuated my forefinger and thumb through two slats in the closed metallic white horizontal miniblinds. Through the gap in the blinds I peeked at her driving her black BMW past the ficus tree and the flame-colored bougainvillea on my condo's frontage.

She drove down San Vicente Boulevard. Coral trees studded the median strip that bisected the boulevard. She did not see me.

My head was killing me.

I left the miniblinds. I did more coke. Instead of making me feel better, it seemed to make my head hurt even more. And to top it off, my nose commenced bleeding. Christ, it felt like my brains were melting and dripping through my nostrils. My colleague at my law firm could have sold me strychnine instead of coke for all I knew.

From behind my back the parrot said, "Have a nice day, pervert."

I could not believe my ears. I had distinctly heard the word *pervert*. Who had taught it to say that?

My nose was bleeding all over my white button-down Armani shirt and onto my black-and-white snakeskin boots, as I turned to confront the creature. I half expected to see it laughing at me. The expression on its green feathery face was inscrutable. My eyes, nostrils, and sinuses were burning and my head was throbbing as if on the verge of exploding. I scrutinized the parrot's face. Its face revealed nothing.

"Have a nice day, pervert," the parrot said again.

I started. It was true, then. I had not imagined the parrot's words.

Now I detested the creature. It had the audacity to insult me to my face. I could not stand the sight of it. In two strides I made its cage, opened the wire door, snatched out the squawking, flapping bird, and twisted its neck till the neck snapped and the parrot went limp in my hands.

Sadness welled up inside me as I contemplated the feathery corpse in my hands. Like a shot I threw the parrot down on the floor. I wiped off my hands on my trousers as though that would exonerate me of the bird's death.

I decided it was Mandy's fault that this had happened. Everything had been fine between me and Papagayo till she had arrived here.

I sprayed the parrot with deodorant from an aerosol can so the corpse would not stink. I had no idea how long it took for a parrot's corpse to begin to putrefy. I wrapped the stiff inside a red polystyrene garbage bag. I tied a knot in the top of the bag. Then I drove with the package to the nearest Federal Express office.

Strolling into the office I asked the black clerk there for a packing box. I could see right off the bat that my package would not fit into one of their paper envelopes. I would definitely need a box.

She handed me a collapsed pasteboard box over the counter. I expanded the box. I slid out its flattened cardboard tray, whose sides I raised, and stuffed the garbage bag with the parrot inside it into the tray, which I slid back into the box.

I removed the waxy paper strips that covered the mucilage on the ends of the box. I sealed the pasteboard flaps, thus entombing the parrot.

With a ballpoint pen I filled out the address label. I handed the box to the clerk.

She weighed it on the electronic scale. She told me the cost of the delivery. I charged it to my platinum American Express card. I took a powder, proud of the cool manner in which I had handled the entire affair.

The next morning I awoke with a pounding headache and a ringing in my ears. Realizing it was the phone I got out of bed. I stumbled to the phone on the coffee table. I lifted the handset.

"Hello," I croaked.

"You sick bastard," said Mandy.

"What?"

"You know what I'm talking about!"

"No, I don't."

My mind was logy. I could not think. I could not fathom Mandy's hostility toward me.

"This is the sickest thing I've ever heard of in my life," she said.

I scratched my head. I racked my brains, trying to dope out what she was ranting about. "Are you OK, Mandy?"

"Why you . . . ," she said through her teeth like a dog growling. "Of course I'm not OK. I'm sick to my stomach on account of what you sent me. You pervert."

As I was listening to her I picked up on the parrot's empty cage that stood in the corner of the living room. I recalled as if through a mist my mailing her Papagayo's corpse.

"I'm sorry, Mandy. I didn't mean to offend you."

"Are you kidding? Get your head straight, Bret. This isn't funny. It's sick. It's worse than sick."

"Papagayo died yesterday. I know how fond you were of him so I mailed him to you. I had no intention of upsetting you. I didn't realize . . ."

"What'd he die of?"

"I don't know. He just keeled over. I thought you'd want to know."

"Well, you didn't have to send him to me," she said with disgust, but I could tell from her voice that she was calming down.

"Come on over. I have a present for you."

She hung fire. At last she said, "All right. As long as you're sorry for mailing—"

"I'm sorry. I wasn't thinking."

"I'll see you in about an hour."

We hung up.

Lickety-split I flung on my clothes, shaved, cleaned up, and drove to the pet shop.

When Mandy rapped on my door the better part of an hour later, I answered it. I watched her eyes gape with amazement as she clapped them on me standing there in the doorway with a green macaw perched on my shoulder.

I let her in. I closed the door behind her. "I bought a new one."

She smiled at the parrot. "Hi, parrot."

"Have a nice day, parrot," said the bird.

"He's darling," Mandy told me. Gazing at the parrot she said, "Polly, want a cracker?"

I turned my face to look at the creature. It shifted its talons on my shoulder, digging them through the material of my shirt and into my shoulder so hard that I winced in pain as I felt them drawing blood. The parrot fluttered its Day-Glo green wings in my face, which occasioned me to cough, and, to my shock, I heard it say to me—and the last word, as clear as a bell, made my skin crawl—"Have a nice day, pervert."

I had not taught it to say "pervert." I had not taught it to say anything. I did not have enough time to teach it to say anything. I had just bought it. The owner of the store must have taught it to say, "Have a nice day, pervert." But why would he teach the bird to say that? I wasn't going to waste any time thinking about it.

In any case, when I heard the word *pervert*, I lost it. In a fit of rage I tried to grab the insulting creature but it flew off my shoulder and escaped.

I scoffed up an Eiffel Tower–shaped bronze statuette that stood on the escritoire. I stormed after the parrot, which was fluttering and hopping across the turquoise plush carpet. I raised the statuette over my head to smash the squawking mass of feathers. I was about to strike when Mandy snagged my arm and screamed for me to stop.

I told her it had no right to insult me. I pushed her out of my way, freeing my arm from her grasp.

"What the hell's wrong with you!" she cried. "It's only a stupid parrot. It doesn't even know what it's saying."

"If it's only a stupid parrot you won't mind if I smash its stupid brain to a pulp."

"You're sick, Bret." She looked at me with nauseous eyes.

I wanted to chase the parrot down and bash its skull in, but Mandy annoyed me.

"Why am I sick?" I said. "I bought this parrot to make you happy."

"Killing it won't make me happy."

I could not understand why she was so angry. She looked like she would start cursing me out any second. Her behavior distracted me and I lost track of the parrot.

"Are you happy now?" I asked.

"Why should I be?"

"You let that rotten bird get away."

"Great!" She searched my face with her cornflower blue eyes, which seemed bigger and bluer than ever. "I'm leaving." She stalked toward the front door.

"You just got here."

"You're about to turn this place into a slaughterhouse. Why would I want to stay?"

"I invited you here to have a good time."

"This isn't my idea of a good time."

"Does that mean you don't want the parrot? I bought him for you."

Her hand on the doorknob, she paused. "I don't like these sick games you're playing with me."

"I don't understand. I thought you liked the parrot."

"I do."

"Then why are you so pissed off?"

"Because you just tried to kill it."

I squeezed the statuette harder with my hand. "It shouldn't have insulted me."

It suddenly became quiet. I heard the refrigerator start to hum to life in the kitchen. The phone rang. I did not answer it.

"Aren't you going to answer it?" asked Mandy.

"If it's important, they'll leave a voice mail."

"What's wrong with you?" Peering at my face she shook her head in bafflement.

"It shouldn't have insulted me."

"A parrot doesn't know what it's saying. Its words are meaningless. They're just sounds."

Disgusted, she opened the door and left.

I walked to the closed miniblinds. I prodded open two metal slats with my fingers. I peeked through the gap. I watched her stalk off, climb into her black BMW, and drive away.

It was that lousy bird's fault. The statuette in my hand, I left the window and went looking for the little dweeb. It wasn't hard to find. I heard it squawking in the kitchen. I picked up on it lurching across the kitchen floor. The parrot's talons clacked against the linoleum tiles.

"Come here, sweetie," I said.

"Come here, pervert," it replied.

That was the last straw. I swung the base of the statuette against the parrot's green head and heard its skull make a muffled cracking sound. All those feathers had probably deadened the sound of the parrot's skull splitting open. The parrot fell dead on the spot.

I laid the parrot out in an empty shoebox.

My head started aching again. I snorted more lines on the kitchen table.

When I was through, I took the parrot out of the shoebox and sprayed the cadaver with deodorant. Then I dumped the parrot into a polystyrene trash bag. I took it to the Fed Ex office.

I slept late the next day and was woken by the incessant ringing of the phone. I rolled out of bed. I caught up the handset of the phone on the coffee table.

I said hello into the handset.

"You sick son of a bitch," Mandy hissed.

"What's wrong?"

"What's wrong?" she mocked.

"Well?"

"I got your package in the mail." She sounded fit to be tied. "I can't believe you'd stoop to doing this again."

"Doing what?" I was still half-asleep. I had trouble concentrating.

"Killing the parrot and sending it to me. What the hell are you trying to prove! If you hate me why don't you just say so, instead of doing this sick stuff?"

"I didn't kill the parrot."

"It's dead, Bret," she blurted. Her voice cracked. She started crying. "It's right over there on the couch."

"I didn't kill it. It flew out of my condo and got run over by a car."

"That's no reason to send it to me." She was sobbing now and making little puling sounds.

"I know how you liked him. I wanted you to see how pretty he was even after he died."

"You really are sick."

"I did it because I love you."

"I have a good mind to call the police."

"For what? What did I do illegal?"

"You're harassing me."

Now it was my turn to get angry. I paced around the room. I yelled into the transmitter, "I sent you the parrot because you like him!"

"I'm not talking to you anymore." With that, she slammed down the handset. It made a loud click.

I would have to make amends to her. I knew just how to do it.

*

Two hours later I was standing at the front door to her condo ringing her doorbell, holding a cage with a new green macaw in it.

She cracked her door and peeked at me over the chain-lock that stretched tight between the door and the jamb.

"What do you want?" she demanded.

"I'm sorry for what I did. I bought you a parrot."

She made to close the door, but something held her back. I could see she was looking at the bird and taking a shine to it. Her eyes were lighting up.

"It's for me?" she said, apprehensive after what had happened to the other two parrots.

"Yes."

She still seemed reluctant to undo the chain-lock and let me in.

"Don't you like him?" I asked, sounding worried.

"Yes. He's cute."

"He's all yours."

I sensed she was mulling it over. Of two minds she finally decided to let me into her condo.

As soon as I walked in and she closed the door, I opened the cage and let the parrot flutter out. It strutted across the floor, feeling its legs and trying out its wings.

"Why'd you do that?" asked Mandy, but I could tell she wasn't angry.

I knew she hated seeing animals locked in cages as much as I did.

"He wanted to be free," I said.

When the bird heard my voice, it said, "Have a nice day, pervert."

I saw red. That was the thanks I got for freeing the turd maker. I wanted to wring its scrawny neck. I glowered at its dead-looking doll's eyes.

"What's wrong?" asked Mandy.

"Did you hear what it said to me?"

"All it did was squawk."

"Squawk—*schmuawk*. You heard what it called me. You know I can't stand being insulted in front of you."

"Chill out. Let's not have another scene. I knew I shouldn't have let you in."

"Come off it, Mandy. You know how much you dig our little scenes. They make you hot."

"You're taking this parrot thing too far."

She was wearing a sheer flamingo pink peignoir tied loosely about her narrow waist. When she moved, her robe shifted and I could see she wasn't wearing a bra.

"You know you like it when we fight and then we make up later," I said. "You get off on it. It's your competitive drive you need for showbiz. You need to feel your conquering someone when you go to bed with them."

"Speak for yourself."

I could see I had touched a nerve. "You know you get excited by our games. Our bodies are so hot now, we can hardly keep our hands off each other."

I was convinced she responded by a subtle movement of her body designed to widen the opening in her peignoir in order to reveal more of the swell of her full breasts.

As I fixed to move toward Mandy, that damned parrot jumped up and fluttered its wings in my face, slapping my cheeks with a lot more strength than I gave it credit for. It was like somebody snapping a sheet in my face over and over, whacking and stinging my cheeks, reddening my face.

Pulling away from the parrot I swatted at it. It dodged my blow and retreated, squawking.

"Have a nice day, pervert," it said.

Was the pet-shop owner training all these parrots to disrespect me? Why else would they be saying the same insult to me?

I despised the parrot for humiliating me in front of Mandy. It was then that I remembered the meat cleaver I had brought with me, which I had secreted between my waistband and my stomach behind my silk moiré jacket. I would lop off the bird's head in front of Mandy's very eyes.

When she saw me remove the meat cleaver from my trousers, she went ballistic.

She screamed at me, "No!" She had lost all control of herself. She charged me.

I put the loaded and fastened polystyrene trash bag in the backseat of my Jag XJS. I drove away form Mandy's condo toward Malibu. I felt more or less relieved but my head was killing me and I had trouble concentrating as I made for the Fed Ex office.

Why did my head always ache? Why couldn't Mandy get it through her head how much I loved her? How many times did I have to prove it to her? How many parrots did I have to buy? She just did not get it.

The sky was a cloudless azure. I smelled the sweet scent of frangipani in the air beneath the motionless palms that arched upward.

What was wrong with my head? Why couldn't I remember anything?

My thoughts were interrupted by a siren. I glanced in the rearview mirror and saw a CHP officer riding on a motorcycle motioning for me to pull over, his red and blue lights flashing.

I turned onto the shoulder and parked. I had no idea what was up.

Dressed in a butternut uniform and a pair of black jackboots, the helmeted stone-faced CHP cop pulled up behind me. He dismounted from his Yamaha motorcycle. He swaggered up to me, his barrel chest thrust out.

"You were doing ninety," he said under his breath. "Could I please see your driver's license, sir?"

I dug my hand-tooled leather wallet out of my silk moiré jacket's breast pocket. I handed the wallet to him.

"Just the driver's license, sir," he said.

Shrugging, I obliged him.

As I watched him read my license I heard a scream from the backseat.

The cop heard it too and, raising his head from his reading, glared at me. "What?"

"I didn't say anything."

He resumed reading my license.

Another scream, this one louder than before.

He started at the sound.

"All right, sir. Please step out of the car," he said, his hand moving toward the butt of the service revolver snug in the leather holster on his hip.

Gingerly, I slid out of my car, staggered by what was happening, my mind spinning.

And there it was again. A third earsplitting ungodly scream.

Only this time, watching me the cop could see I wasn't the one doing the screaming. He looked in the backseat where I had stored the trash bag. In horror, I could only stand and watch as I saw the trash bag move. The cop saw it too. It skidded an inch on the Corinthian leather of the backseat.

He drew his gun. Holding it trained on me, he withdrew the trash bag from the backseat.

Hell, I thought, as he set the bag on the Jaguar's hood. I watched him undo the black plastic zip tie that secured the bag's neck. He was having difficulty undoing the zip tie with one hand because he was holding his gun leveled at me at the same time with the other. He managed to undo the zip tie.

At that moment there was a bloodcurdling shriek as Mandy's head flew out of the bag, her eyes staring into infinity, her bloody mouth a rictus of fear. The green parrot fluttered out frantically from behind her into my face, saying—

A cool sea breeze freshened as I put the head back into the ripped polystyrene bag. The parrot's beak must have torn the plastic as the parrot flew out of the bag. In any case, I wondered how I was going to carry the head to the Fed Ex office, what with the condition of the bag.

The highway patrolman kind of smiled at me and took my hand, as if to say that everything was going to be all right. The thing is, he did not know that I had to take the bag to the Fed Ex office.

I had this image of us walking hand in hand down the beach as the guava sun set and the strumming surf crashed at our feet.

He seemed like a nice man. Maybe I could explain to him about the important shipment I had to send to Mandy. I had found something very dear to her that she had lost. I wanted to make sure she got it back.

"Do you have any aspirin?" I asked him.

Blindman's Buff

Billings knew it was two o'clock. He felt the familiar triangle of sunlight warm the back of his right hand. He heard the cars whooshing continuously monotonously past his apartment's window.

It was time for his walk. Had he been dozing? Billings wondered. Had he been slurping tomato soup a moment ago or had he dreamt it? It was difficult to concentrate. The noise of the endless cars disquieted him.

He could hear a television soap opera prattling incoherently from a neighbor's room. He distinctly remembered eating tomato soup. Yet he felt hungry. A part of his mind exhorted him to eat lunch. Another part argued that he had already eaten. He seemed to feel hungry, but maybe that was the dream.

Billings knew it was time to walk Edgar, his Alsatian, because Billings felt the sunlight warming the back of his hand. He arose from his wingchair. He heard Edgar's paws clicking against the floor tiles as Edgar approached him.

As always at this time, Edgar chomped the leather leash between his moist fangs. Billings removed the leash from Edgar's mouth. Billings attached the leash's metal spring-lock to Edgar's leather collar. Billings groped for his cane in the corner of the room. He donned his electrician's cap. It reminded him of his profession when he had two healthy eyes. Edgar led him out the door.

They walked through the carpeted corridor to the concrete steps leading to the sidewalk. They paused on the landing. A cool fitful ocean breeze from Santa Monica brushed his face.

"Oh, hello, Mr. Billings," said Mrs. De Pasquale.

He recognized her instantly from her squawking voice. She lived in the apartment across the hall from his.

"Hello," he said.

He heard crumpling paper. He smelled fresh apples. She must have been carrying groceries, he decided.

"Do you need any help?" she asked.

"No."

She always asked him that. He couldn't stand it. Did he look like he needed help? he wondered. Probably. He wasn't a helpless baby, though. He could take care of himself. He always had. He had to. There weren't many Mrs. De Pasquales you could count on in your times of need in this world. He had learned that the hard way. He had also learned to live with his handicap.

"All right, then," she said. "Be careful walking down the steps." Billings heard the direction of her voice change. "Hello, Edgar," she said.

Billings heard her shift the paper grocery bag in her arms.

He nodded as though he was heeding her advice.

Precariously, he descended the steps. He had little control over his limbs. He had just enough to get by. His cane helped.

A heavy odor of perfume wafted into his nostrils. He knew it was an old woman wearing it. Old women drowned themselves in perfume. Young women daubed it on.

The old woman passed him. She breathed laboriously. She had to be fat, he decided. She wore heavy black shoes. Her fallen nylons bunched in rolls at her ankles. It was true he could not see her, but he liked to imagine how people looked. She wore a light cotton print dress. She worked as a maid. He giggled to himself as he painted his picture of her in his mind.

He walked Edgar toward the bus bench. Jujubes stuck to his soles. He remembered threading his way as a kid through narrow aisles in air-conditioned movie theaters, stepping on Jujubes.

He reclined on the bench. Its sun-baked enamel paint warmed him. He heard two pairs of quick light steps behind him. They had to be children who attended the elementary school behind him. The elementary school had a chain-link fence around it. Billings knew the fence was there because he had heard the fence jingle many times when schoolchildren in the schoolyard played with it.

Right now one of the two children standing behind the fence was unwrapping a candy bar or a snack food. Billings couldn't be sure which.

"He stinks like a gas station toilet," said one of the children.

The other child laughed. They scurried away. Billings could not tell if they were boys or girls from their voices.

He heard Edgar's claws clicking against the sidewalk.

A fire engine's siren obliterated all other sounds. The siren's scream deafened him. He felt as though somebody was stuffing pillows in his ears for about a minute. Edgar's leash tensed in Billings's arthritic hand. Where was Edgar trying to go? wondered Billings. Had he spotted a cat? The leash relaxed.

Someone sat beside Billings on the bench. The bench creaked under the person's weight. A prospective passenger, decided Billings. He smelled rank underarm sweat and beer. His neighbor must be a young man. Billings heard a brief slight scraping. Something hissed and cackled. He smelled acrid sulfur. A garbage truck grunted by. He smelled oranges. That garbage truck always smelled of sickly sweet oranges. It passed him every Wednesday at this time. He sniffed. Cigarette smoke stung the back of his throat. The young man had lit a match and was now smoking a cigarette. Billings heard him impatiently tapping his leather-soled shoe against the sidewalk.

Billings heard a transistor radio approaching. A jogger panted by in exhaustion. The radio newscaster's static-laced voice tailed off as the jogger departed. A car screeched to a halt for the nearby traffic light. The twang of electric guitars from blaring rock music lashed the air.

"Fuck you, old man," a teenager muttered indistinctly through the caterwauling guitars.

Billings heard the car race away. The music was drowned out by internal-combustion engines roaring like combing waves. A foreign car honked shrilly. He could tell it was foreign because of the horn's tone.

"I'm gonna rob you tonight, you old creep," the young man sitting beside him whispered into his ear. "Leave your door open, or I'll kill you."

Billings heard the young man's heels clack off into the internal-combustion sea.

A foul pungent taste like vomit filled Billings's mouth. He didn't know what to do. Should he call the police? he wondered. Should he tell Mrs. De Pasquale? No. Hadn't he prided himself on telling everyone he wasn't a helpless baby? This was his problem. He had to take care of it himself. He could do it. He would prove he was still a man.

He listened to Edgar urinate against the chain-link fence. Somebody or something scrounged in the nearby grated metal wastebasket. It had to be Herb Guffy, decided Billings.

"Hi, Herb," said Billings.

The scrounging stopped.

"Hi," Herb replied heartily.

Guffy always pawed through the wastebaskets to retrieve aluminum soda cans. He sold the aluminum cans he collected to a recycling plant. He lived next door to Billings. They shared a bathroom between their apartments. They shared everything in that bathroom. They even shared Guffy's athlete's foot. Billings always knew when Guffy entered the bathroom. Guffy would curse his catheter at the toilet.

Should he tell Guffy about the young man's threat? Billings wondered.

"Did you see a young man beside me a few minutes ago?" Billings asked.

"No," answered Guffy.

Guffy resumed rooting through the garbage.

Billings returned to his apartment. He tottered with Edgar down the sidewalk.

Billings entered his apartment. He locked the door behind him. That was no good, he decided. If the bandit found the door locked, it would infuriate him. The bandit would as like as not break in through the window and kill him.

Billings would have to leave the door unlocked for the crook. How could he fight someone he could not see? Billings wondered. Billings shuffled toward his closet. He reached for the top shelf. He withdrew a Colt .45 automatic from behind a hatbox.

He felt the automatic's wooden crosshatched stock. A .45 would stop that punk cold. The trouble was, Billings knew, how could he aim at someone he could not see?

Leaning over he felt around the floor. He plucked a loaded magazine from a moldering leather hiking boot on the closet floor. He slapped the magazine into the automatic. He had never fired the gun. He never cleaned it. He hoped it would not jam. How could he aim it? he wondered.

He located a skein of twine in his desk. He unwound a length of the twine. He severed it from the skein with his penknife. He looped the twine. He sliced the end of the loop with his penknife to form two equal lengths of string.

He didn't know the color of the string. He assumed it was white. He remembered he stored a bottle of black shoe polish in his closet. He retrieved the bottle. He smeared shoe polish on the two lengths of twine with a Kleenex.

He walked to the front door. He stood with his back flush against the closed door. He walked in a beeline away from the door. He groped for his wingchair. He found it. He slid it across the floor to a spot directly in front of the door. He conjectured it was about seven feet from the door.

He pulled a package of thumbtacks from his desk drawer. He removed two tacks from their pasteboard cushion. He tacked the end of one of the lengths of string to the doorjamb near the doorknob. He tacked the end of the other string at the same height to the opposite doorjamb.

He attached the free ends of the string to the trigger frame of his .45. He backed deliberately from the door to his wingchair. He felt the cords become taut. The chair was too far away. He slid it closer to the door. He sat facing the unlocked door. He now had the automatic trained at the center of the door.

He calculated the crook was about his height from the angle at which the crook had whispered in his ear. They seemed to be level with each other while they had been sitting on the bus bench. The doorknob reached to Billings's stomach. If he aimed one foot higher, he would be aiming at the bandit's chest, Billings decided. Billings tilted the automatic upward.

The twine centered the gun on the door. The shoe polish camouflaged the twine, so the bandit could not discern it in the dark. There were no lights in the room. What was the point of having lights when he could not see? he wondered. He didn't need lights. Only people who could see needed lights.

He waited.

It must have been dark by now. It had taken him a few hours to coat the strings with shoe polish. He had to scrupulously feel the twine to make certain he had coated it completely. He felt hungry. His stomach gurgled. Billings dared not prepare his frozen dinner. The crook might break in while Billings ate it.

Billings clutched the automatic's stock tensely in his palsied hand.

Footfalls creaked down the corridor. He held his breath in anticipation. He heard his doorknob turning. He prepared to squeeze the trigger.

"Damn," the voice slurred drunkenly. "Where the hell am I?"

The drunk staggered from the door.

Billings breathed a sigh of relief. What if he had shot that drunkard by mistake? he wondered. What if Mrs. De Pasquale entered his room, or Herb Guffy? What if he shot them by mistake? How would he know if the person entering his apartment was really the crook? Sweat beaded on his craggy forehead. His heart pounded in apprehension.

Was the beery young man with the rancid armpits real? Billings wondered. Had Billings imagined him? Guffy had not seen the young man. Billings still could not recall if he had eaten tomato soup for lunch. Had he dozed on the bus bench and dreamt the reeking young man smoking a cigarette?

Sweat oozed in droplets over Billings's upper lip. Maybe he should phone the police. He didn't stand a chance against a crook who could see him. Why did he have to act like a stubborn old fool by taking care of this problem himself? Billings wondered. Mrs. De Pasquale frequently chided him for his senile obstinacy. Maybe she was right.

He really should phone the police, he decided. What if the crook came while he dialed the telephone? Anyway he didn't know the police department's phone number. That was no excuse, he told himself. He could always dial 9-1-1.

He heard the metal door latch snick. His violently fluttering heart yearned to fly out its bony cage. Somebody was opening the door! What if it was Mrs. De Pasquale? Billings wondered. Billings's index finger gently squeezed the automatic's trigger. What if it was Herb Guffy? How could Billings tell who it was? The door creaked open softly.

Billings had to make up his mind in short order. If he waited any longer, it would be too late. The bandit would escape Billings's line of fire. If that happened, Billings would have no idea where to aim. He swallowed apprehensively. What to do? he wondered.

Mrs. De Pasquale wouldn't enter his room without identifying herself, Billings decided. She would never do that. Neither would Herb Guffy. It had to be the bandit. Billings felt human heat radiating through the apartment.

He fired the automatic twice. The explosion of the gun shocked Billings's eardrums. He recoiled in pain. The .45-caliber bullets easily penetrated the deal door. He heard splintering wood. Somebody groaned. Billings jerked the trigger a third time at the sound of the groan.

The automatic jammed. Billings strained his ears to hear what happened next. A body thumped in a heap against the hall floor. Silence for a moment. Feet dragged heavily against the corridor carpet. The footfalls headed toward the apartment house's lobby. The bandit remained alive, but Billings had defeated him.

Billings didn't know what to do now. He sighed with relief. He had scared the bandit off. Didn't anyone hear the shots? Billings wondered. Why didn't anyone knock at his door to check up on him? They were probably too frightened. Who could blame them? He didn't need them anyway. He had won!

With a start he heard his window squeal open in its wooden frame. Edgar barked.

"Quiet, Edgar," whispered Billings.

Billings couldn't hear the bandit move with Edgar barking. Whining for a second, Edgar obeyed Billings and stopped barking. Billings needed absolute quiet in order to hear the whereabouts of the bandit.

The bandit must be crawling through the window, decided Billings. Billings fired his .45 in the direction of the window. The gun was still jammed. He cursed.

He was helpless. His tremulous hand tightened its grip on his cane. He listened intently. The bandit sounded as if he was tumbling into the room. He thudded against the floor. He groaned on impact.

Billings must have wounded him. Should he scream for help? wondered Billings. No. The bandit would locate him from the direction of his scream. At the moment, the bandit could not know where Billings was now. The room was pitch-black, which put Billings and the crook on equal footing, Billings knew. They were doing battle on a level playing field. In fact, Billings may have had a slight advantage thanks to the extra sensitivity of his sense of hearing, which had sharpened after he had lost his sight.

Billings heard the bandit stumble against Billings's escritoire.

"You'll die for this, old man," the bandit hissed. "Come out where I can see you. It's no use hiding."

Billings had to get inside the crook's mind. Billings had to know exactly where the crook stood, so he could cudgel the crook. The crook made no noise. Was he tiptoeing somewhere? Billings wondered. Where?

Billings realized the answer. The bandit wanted to gain the upper hand. He had to be making for the light switch, Billings decided. That was the logical move for a man who needed light.

If Billings wanted to find a light switch in a stranger's apartment, where would he look? Near the door, Billings decided. Most apartments had light switches near the door frame for you to flick on as you entered the room.

Billings lunged for the door. He bludgeoned the crook with his shillelagh-like cane. To Billings it felt like he was striking the bandit's head and back. Something burned Billings's wrist. Billings felt warm fluid trickle from his wrist. Billings decided the fluid was his blood.

A metal object clattered against the floor. The bandit's knife? Billings wondered. Billings heard a body slump against the doorjamb.

Police sirens cried desultory falsetto shrieks down the street.

"Are you OK, Mr. Billings?" Mrs. De Pasquale whimpered through Billings's bullet-shattered door.

"I'm bleeding a bit. That's all."

"Hail Mary, Mother of God," she lamented. "That little thief. Is he gone?" she whispered fearfully.

"He's here on the floor, I think." With his cane Billings could feel a motionless body sprawled in front of him. "Out like a light."

Edgar barked.

"Is Edgar all right?" asked Mrs. De Pasquale.

"Right as rain," said Billings.

"Hail Mary, Mother of God. I phoned the police. What happened?"

"This crook wanted to play blindman's buff with me," said Billings. "He never had a chance. He was playing against a pro."

Smiling, Billings patted Edgar's head. Billings felt Edgar's wet snoot nuzzle the back of his hand in return.

Room 208

Molson wished he liked his job—flipping burgers at Happy Joe's Burger Palace on the UC Playa campus. He wished there was something, *anything* good about his job. He sighed behind the counter.

"I ordered French fries with that," barked the snotty sixteen year old standing in front of the counter.

Molson gave the disgruntled customer a look. Molson wanted to fade into the woodwork.

"Today—*puh-lease*," whined the teenager. He scratched the mucus-coated ring in his nose.

It wasn't working, decided Molson. He wasn't fading anywhere. The guy was still there busting his chops. Drama was the last thing Molson needed. He wasn't in the mood today. He didn't think he was going to last much longer at this job. But money didn't grow on trees.

"I demand to talk to your boss," declared the customer. He jabbed his forefinger against the countertop several times, his face twitching with anger.

Molson glanced at his wristwatch. It was time for him to clock out.

He didn't know how much more of this job he could take. What was wrong with him? Was he the only cashier who felt this way? The other cashiers didn't seem to have problems with the customers. Molson had more than his fair share of abusive customers, it seemed to him.

Fed up, Molson handed the griping teenager a box of French fries and accidentally on purpose dropped them on the floor.

"Do you want ketchup?" asked Molson.

Nonplussed, the teenager hung his mouth open. His face turned white.

Molson tossed two packets of ketchup at him and stalked out of Happy Joe's, probably for the last time. Once the boss heard about this episode from the irate customer, Molson's termination would be a done deal.

Then what would he do? wondered Molson. Without a job, without income, he would be in worse shape than ever. Why was his life spiraling downward after he had graduated from college? He had a BA degree in Philosophy. If he couldn't do better than the McJobs he had been getting, he deserved to be a homeless bum. What would Camus and Nietzsche think of him?

He walked past a campus bulletin board that skirted the sidewalk. He perused the want ads thumbtacked to the cork, casting around for a job.

He picked up on an ad for volunteers for a Psych experiment. It paid fifteen dollars an hour. Not bad, he decided. Almost twice what he was making at Happy Joe's.

He sensed rather than saw eyes staring at him from behind. He turned around.

A middle-aged man was strolling down the other side of the street. He showed no interest in Molson. Yet Molson was certain he had felt eyes on his back.

He shrugged. He turned back to the Psych ad. He memorized the address of the experiment. He would look into it. How could it be worse than flipping burgers till kingdom come? he wondered.

The very idea of returning to work at Happy Joe's drove him batty. He would go stark raving mad if he had to work there another minute. In any case, after Molson's incident there today, it was inconceivable that the boss would allow him back.

Molson decided to sign up for the Psych experiment on the spot. He had nothing else to do and there might be a crowd of applicants for the experiment. After all, the job market was flat and this gig looked like easy money. If he dawdled, he might lose out on the job. The location of the experiment was within walking distance. He knew that much. He had graduated from UC Playa a couple years ago. He set out for the address of the experiment at a brisk clip.

His sojourn at the university was the zenith of his life compared to what he was going through now. You went to class. You studied. You passed your courses. You graduated. Some of the courses were interesting. Some weren't.

Then you went out into the real world. You got bottom-feeder jobs. You sucked up. You worked like a horse. You got treated like dirt. You got paid squat.

What the hell happened? Molson wondered. Wasn't a college degree supposed to guarantee its bearer a good, high-paying job? That was the spin put out by the universities, anyway. Then again, the universities were in it for the money just like everybody else. That being the case, how could you trust anything they said?

Molson kept walking.

He found the Warren Psychology Building. Things hadn't changed much since he had attended college. Students were making out on the brick steps of the building. Others were idling around, in no particular hurry to attend their next class.

Molson made his way to the room of the experiment. Room 208. Its wooden door was closed.

He saw the list of volunteers for the experiment posted on the door. He withdrew a ballpoint pen from his trouser pocket. He signed up.

"You made a good decision," a voice from behind him said.

Molson started. He whirled around.

A middle-aged man was standing, facing him. Molson could not be sure if it was the same guy that he had seen when he had first spotted the ad on the bulletin board along the sidewalk. That guy had been too far away at the time for Molson to discern his face clearly. In any case, this guy's face was bland, unremarkable.

"We've had our eyes on you," said the generic man. "We think you're one of us."

"One of whom?" asked Molson.

"You'll see."

Who was this guy? Molson wondered. Was he just a bullshit artist?

"Do I know you?" asked Molson.

"We've never been introduced, no." The man paused. "Walk right in. You're next." He retreated toward the stairwell. "We knew you'd show up sooner or later."

Molson had no interest in pursuing this incomprehensible conversation with the amazing Cryptoman.

Molson knocked on the door to room 208.

A bespectacled student opened the door. "Are you here to volunteer for the experiment?"

"Yeah."

"I thought so." The student wore blue jeans and a button-down white shirt open at the collar. He handed Molson a pencil and an application form. "Have a seat and fill out this form, please. We've been expecting you."

More cryptic hooey, decided Molson. Expecting him, indeed. Maybe this was the first phase of the experiment. *Make the volunteer believe he's been under observation by this group that's administering the test*, Molson thought. But what was the point?

Molson accepted the form and the pencil. He sat in one of the deal chairs lined up against the wall. One of the chair's legs was shorter than the rest, he noticed as he sat down and rocked a bit. He proceeded to fill out the form. The bespectacled student sat at a metal desk.

Finished with the form, Molson walked over to the student and handed it to him.

The student smiled. He looked over the completed form. "By the way, my name is Bill. I'll check this out and I'll be right with you." He nodded to the chairs. "Have a seat."

Molson returned to his lopsided chair. He didn't have long to wait.

Bill approached him. "You've been approved. Let's go."

Molson followed him to a closed door. Bill opened the door. He led Molson into a small, sparsely lit windowless room. The room was empty save for a wooden chair in the middle of the floor and a machine of some sort that sat on a table beside the chair. Molson didn't like the looks of this. What kind of experiment had he signed up for? he wondered.

Bill caught him scoping out the machine. "It's a cardiotachometer. It measures your pulse and respiration."

"Why?"

"We need this information for the experiment." Bill smiled. "Relax. You won't feel a thing. Have a seat."

Molson wondered what he was getting into. He demurred. He was starting to feel regrets about signing up for this experiment. On the other hand, it couldn't be any worse than Happy Joe's, and he needed the money.

He sat down.

Bill strapped Molson's arms to the chair's wooden armrests. Molson noted that the chair's legs were bolted to the linoleum floor with angle irons. Not a good sign, he decided.

"Why the straps?" he asked.

"This is a delicate instrument. We don't want you moving your arms while the electrodes are taped to them."

"Why would I want to move my arms?" Molson asked suspiciously.

Bill smiled. "It's just a precaution. You might move your arms reflexively. That would spoil the experiment. We can't have that."

Bill was doing a lot of smiling, Molson noticed. All the smiles weren't making Molson feel comfortable, if their intent was to comfort. In fact, they were having the opposite effect. He found them disconcerting.

"I guess not," said Molson.

Bill made to leave the room. "Oh, we'll be filming and recording everything you say and do.

There's a one-way mirror over there." He gestured toward the looking glass on the wall.

Molson glanced at the mirror. "You didn't say anything about filming me."

"It was in that form you signed. I thought you read it. By signing it, you granted us permission to conduct the experiment on you. You also authorized us to film your reactions here."

Molson had not read the fine print. He had merely skimmed the document.

"As long as you don't sell the film on the Internet," Molson deadpanned.

Bill smiled. "No. The film won't be made public."

Molson heard the door shut and he knew he was alone in the room.

Startling him, a bright light came on and shone directly in his face, blinding him. Molson squinted. When his eyes became accustomed to the light, he could make out the lens of a movie camera poking through the wall in front of him. He had not noticed a hole in the wall there before. The hole must have been covered up or camouflaged somehow.

Shadowy figures floated and melded behind the one-way mirror above the light. Molson could not make out any actual human shapes. The light was aimed right in his eyes.

"Relax," a disembodied, mellifluous voice said.

"Easy for you to say."

"This is just a psychology experiment," said the soothing voice.

Molson had not anticipated being strapped to this uncomfortable chair when he signed up for this experiment. The chair reminded him of an electric chair, no less. How could he relax manacled to this contraption? he wondered.

"As briefly as possible, give us your ethos," said the voice.

"My what?" Molson wasn't familiar with the term *ethos*.

"Your philosophy of life."

Oh, great. One of those *tests*, Molson thought. He should have expected as much in an experiment in a college environment. The what-is-the-meaning-of-life question every college kid ponders at one time or another. What bugged him was he should have known the meaning of the word *ethos*. After all, he was a Philosophy major.

He could have come up with an answer from Schopenhauer, or Nietzsche, or Plato, or a host of other philosophers. The truth of the matter was none of their answers satisfied him.

"Live and let live," Molson said at last, racking his brains to come up with an answer.

The voice laughed caustically. "Do you honestly think anyone can live like that?"

The brutal, derisive laugh caught Molson off guard. What had happened to the soothing voice that had greeted him? he wondered. What was going on here?

"Yeah," he mumbled.

"What if America had thought that way during World War II? Hitler and his Nazis would have conquered the world. Your philosophy is idiotic. No wonder you're a loser."

"I gave you my answer. What more do you want?" Molson felt his heart accelerating.

"Your answer's pathetic. You're pathetic. A loser."

"I don't have to listen to this."

"Like hell you don't." The voice paused a beat. "Do you have a girlfriend?"

"No," Molson muttered.

"Why not?"

"I haven't met—"

"Because you're a loser. That's why not. Don't give me a rationalization."

"What's my personal life got to do with anything?"

"It's got everything to do with this test. There are several reasons you don't have a girlfriend."

Molson felt his face reddening. Here he was being treated like dirt again, and there was nothing he could do about it. It was like being back with the disgruntled teenager at Happy Joe's. Molson had to sit here and take it. He struggled to free his arms from the straps that bound him. *The sons of bitches behind that one-way mirror!* he thought. He was dying to take a swing at them.

"Show your faces, you cowards!" he cried. "Or don't you have the guts?"

"Shut up. One reason you don't have a girlfriend is because of that crappy car you drive around in. A 1967 Beetle—that's what your application says here."

"I could care less if you don't like my car."

"No good-looking babe in her right mind would set foot in a hunk of junk like that."

"Bite me!"

"Witty retort," said the voice dryly. "Another reason you don't have a girl is because your dong's too short."

Furious, Molson was flushing again.

"Women can't stand a guy with a dong that's under a foot long," the voice went on.

Now it was Molson's turn to laugh. "Is that what your mother told you?"

"Haven't you ever seen porno flicks? The girls can't get turned on unless the guy's got a dick at least a foot long."

"Why doesn't she just use a baseball bat?"

"If you don't believe me, where's your girlfriend?"

"What is this? Are you recruiting porn stars?"

"Don't answer a question with a question."

"Says who?" Molson wondered who these guys were. They didn't sound like a bunch of fuddy-duddy professors to him.

"Then where's your girlfriend?" the voice said calmly.

"Who wants to know?"

Molson hated himself for blushing and sweating profusely when they were grilling him—and, to his chagrin, it had all been caught on film in living color. He would never be able to live down the shame if somebody got ahold of the film.

It wasn't over yet.

"Or maybe," the voice purred. "Maybe you're a closet case."

"Or maybe you are. You haven't even got the *cojones* to show your face, twerp."

At this point, the needles on the cardiotachometer must have been flying off the charts, Molson figured. He wanted to step outside with the "Voice" and wring his neck.

Once again, Molson struggled to break free from his bonds. To no avail. He felt the cords in his neck stiffen as he strained against the leather. The straps around his arms would not budge.

His sadistic tormenters were crippling him psychologically. He was at their mercy.

"You're an antisocial misfit who is quite possibly psychotic," said the voice.

"Psycho this!" burst Molson.

"The reason you can't hold a job is because you hate your jobs. Your employers pick up on that, and they fire you. Who the hell wants a disgruntled employee moping around?"

"Then why don't *you* fire me and let me the hell out of this dump?"

"Because we're not done with you."

"What are you trying to tell me?"

"You'll leave when we're good and ready to tell you to leave."

"And then I'm gonna hurl this chair through that one-way mirror you're hiding behind."

"No. You won't."

"Then you don't know me very well."

"We know you better than you know yourself."

Molson sniggered. "Then why won't I throw this chair in your face?"

The bright lights dimmed a fraction.

"Because you're one of us," said the voice.

Molson was incredulous.

"We're misfits too," the voice went on. "Losers, if you will. We're members of a CIA cadre called the 'Fellowship.' We're unhappy with the way things are going in the U.S. of A. We're as pissed off as you are, and now we know—because of this experiment—that you have what it takes to be one of us, that is, a full-fledged member of our cadre."

"What is it that I have?" Molson asked, not buying in to the voice's explanation.

"You have inside you the ability to take out a fellow human being."

Molson couldn't believe his ears. The way he saw it, this experiment was getting more whacked out by the minute. "Am I hearing you right?"

"We have come to the conclusion that the only way to win in our current degenerate high-tech society is to blow away our enemies. Our mission is to right the wrongs, and, in the process, flip our corrupt society on its head."

"That's a tall order."

"Every journey begins with the first step."

"Trope." Where was this nutcase experiment going? Molson wondered.

"We must rid ourselves of the cancer known as technocracy. It's turning individuals into machines. Technology is not working for us as it was designed to do. Instead, it's enslaving us. We Americans are a people who don't have the faintest idea who we are anymore."

"Let's cut to the chase. Why do you think I subscribe to your philosophy?"

"It's either that or you go on being a loser for the rest of your life, stuck in brain-dead beast-of-burden jobs that give you no satisfaction."

"Let's get on with it."

The movie camera was shut off.

"We want you to take out the president of this misguided university," said the voice, "and make him suffer, goddamn it."

"Why should I?"

"Does a hundred thousand dollars sound like a good reason?"

Molson nodded. "Yeah."

At that moment, for Molson, the lights went out, figuratively as well as literally. He never knew what hit him. All he could remember later was that he saw a bright white flash and felt a sharp blow to his head.

*

The next day, Molson woke up. With a headache. He sat on the edge of his bed for a moment, waiting for the pain to subside.

He didn't want to get up but he had work to do.

He slipped on a pair of deerskin driving gloves. He tucked his Heckler & Koch P30 9 mm automatic inside his waistband. He wore a lightweight black jacket to shield the pistol from view. He took the bus to the university. He didn't want anyone to see his car parked on campus that day.

He got off the bus on the campus. He angled for the administrative building. He had no trouble entering the building and making his way to the president's office.

There were no security guards, Molson noticed. Why should there be? Why would anyone want to kill a university president?

The only thing that concerned Molson was his escape. The actual kill should be no problem.

He walked to the president's office. The door was open. His brunette secretary was sitting at her desk, typing on her computer.

Molson strolled by the office without drawing her attention. He picked up on a pay phone at the end of the corridor. He approached the phone. He withdrew a tattered, musty phonebook from the ledge it occupied under the phone. He found the phone number for the president's office in the phone book. Molson lifted the black plastic receiver. The receiver in his hand, he slotted quarters into the phone. He punched out the number.

The president's secretary answered on the third ring. "President Chemsak's office."

"Hello," said Molson. "This is UPS. We have a package for your office here."

"Come on up," she said.

"I'd like to, but the front door's locked."

"It's not supposed to be locked. You can leave the package there at the door, if you want. I'll get it later."

"No, I can't do that, ma'am. I need your signature."

"Oh. OK. I'll be right down."

"Thanks, ma'am."

Molson heard her hang up. He hung up. He watched her leave her office and head down the hall. When she disappeared from view he made sure the corridor was empty then strode toward the president's office.

Molson walked into the secretary's office. He angled through it. He opened the door to President Chemsak's inner office.

Chemsak was sitting at a large wooden desk, much larger than his secretary's. To Molson he looked fiftysomething. Chemsak sported grizzled whiskers and wore horn-rimmed spectacles. When he looked up from the document he was reading and saw Molson, he blinked twice in surprise. He obviously wasn't expecting company, decided Molson. Was he expecting to be shot? Probably not.

Molson pulled his H&K P30 out of his waistband and put two rounds through Chemsak's head.

Chemsak didn't have time to blink again. The impetus of the two 9 mm rounds at such close range hurled him back in his padded leather chair, which rolled backward on its plastic casters toward the window. The chair came to a halt on the squeaky casters. Chemsak's head lolled to the left. Spalls of the occipital bone of his bloody skull mixed with brains splattered against the leather upholstery on the seat back.

Molson was out of the office like a shot. He ducked into the corridor's deserted stairwell. He dropped the gun. It was cold. He had bought it a year ago on the black market. The gun was untraceable.

He slipped out a side door to the administration building.

Bill was in room 208 when he found out about the murder in the newspaper the next morning. "Oh, shit."

He disappeared into the empty testing room.

In exasperation, he told the voice, "He believed us."

"Who? What?" said the voice.

At his wit's end, Bill paced frantically around the office.

"Molson," he said, his face florid. "The chowderhead actually believed us. He went and killed the president."

"Oh no! Didn't you tell the idiot it was just a test?"

"Of course. He read and signed the application form."

"It can't be!" cried the voice. "It can't be! What in the world was he thinking? *He really must be a psycho.*" The voice caught his breath. "Did they arrest him?"

"No. Not yet."

"Maybe it wasn't him. It could have been anyone, for all we know."

Bill thought about it. "That's true. How do we know for sure it was him?"

The voice breathed a sigh of relief. "Even if it was him, he can't implicate us, as long as he remains at large." The voice hung fire. "And besides, he never saw my face."

"He saw mine," objected Bill.

"Nobody will believe anything he says. I tell you, he can't implicate us."

The phone rang on the table near the wooden chair.

"Hello," said Bill, lifting the handset to his ear. The blood drained from his face as he listened.

"Who is it?" demanded the voice from behind the one-way mirror.

"That may be the least of our problems."

"What are you babbling about?"

"Listen," said Bill. He flicked on the phone's loudspeaker.

"I have only three words for you," said Molson's voice over the phone line. "Where's my money?"

"Dear God!" cried the voice.

Black Dog

Phyllis Stuart found a black puppy whining on the sidewalk outside her apartment house. She felt sorry for him. She gathered him in her arms. She took him inside her apartment. He might come in handy as a watchdog, she decided. Twice this year her residence in Inglewood, California, had been burglarized.

He seemed like a cute puppy. She petted his head. Maybe poverty had not annealed her heart after all. She was so used to misery, so numbed by it, she feared she had forgotten how to feel.

She lived with her seven-year-old son Matt in a ramshackle apartment that had timeworn ecru paint with holes in it on the walls. Her husband had run out on her six months ago after he had lost his construction job and could not pay the rent. She had to mop the floors in the apartment house to make ends meet. She moonlighted as a babysitter whenever she got the chance.

Freckle-faced Matt took to the puppy instantly and named him Jip. They grew up together for over a year. Jip became huge. He looked like he was already full grown.

When Phyllis knew what had to be done she became despondent.

"What's wrong, Mommy?" asked Matt.

"Jip has to go."

"What do you mean?"

"He eats too much. We can't afford to have a dog."

Matt gazed at her wide-eyed, unable to understand. "But . . ."

"Don't argue with me," she said irritably. "There's nothing I can do about it."

Crestfallen, Matt looked at Jip, who was lying in a corner of the room biting the fur on his belly to stop the fleas from sucking his blood. Jip had grown alarmingly large, even for a Labrador retriever, Phyllis realized.

Sensing Matt staring at him Jip stood up and padded over to him. Mouth open, pink rasher of tongue dangling out, Jip clicked his claws against the linoleum floor. He was unaware that the tiles on the floor did not match. Most of the tiles were yellow. The newer tiles used to replace the worn-out tiles were off-white. The manager had told Phyllis he had no matching yellow tiles left.

Jip didn't give a hang about the tiles. All of his attention was focused on Matt. Gazing expectantly at Matt, Jip stood next to him.

"Don't get rid of him, Mommy," Matt pleaded.

"It's either you or him." She felt horrible saying that to him, but she had to impress upon him the gravity of the situation.

"Why?"

"I can't feed both of you."

"Poor Jip," Matt said. Tearfully, he patted Jip's head.

Jip whimpered. He did not know why. He knew Matt was upset, so something must be wrong.

"I asked around the neighborhood to see if anyone wanted to buy him but nobody does."

"Then we can keep him?"

"No. We'll have to leave him somewhere."

"He'll starve."

She knew he was right. She could not stand the idea of letting Jip starve to death. It would only prolong his agony. She considered drowning him. Looking at his innocent brown eyes she knew she could never bring herself to do that. She would have to think up another way. She never should have taken him off the sidewalk in the first place. This was what happened when you obeyed your heart, she decided. You ended up breaking it.

"We won't let him starve," she said.

"What will you do with him?"

"I'll take him for a ride."

"Why can't we give him away?"

"Nobody wants him, I told you."

If she dropped Jip off at the dog pound, the attendants there might accuse her of cruelty to animals since he looked undernourished. She could not afford to have the ASPCA suing her or bringing charges against her or whatever they did, she decided.

Jip started whining because he had not eaten in several days.

The Korean cabbie that lived in the apartment below Phyllis thudded his broom handle against his ceiling several times to express his annoyance with the noise.

"Be quiet, Jip," said Matt. He stroked Jip's head.

"If we only had money we could move out of this fleabag," she said. "And that good-for-nothing husband . . . ," she grumbled, cursing. "What's the use of complaining? . . . Doesn't change a thing . . . only money . . . no escape from money . . ."

*

That night, after putting Matt to bed, she took a coiled-up length of rope and a penknife from the closet. The rope in her left hand, Jip's leather leash in her right, she headed with Jip to her car parked on the street. She summoned him into the front seat of her yellow Honda.

She drove him to a dark winding canyon road in the Santa Monica Mountains. Jip happily licked the windshield. He liked riding in cars.

Phyllis parked her Honda on a dirt shoulder beside a thicket of scrub pines. There wasn't much of a moon out. A sprinkling of stars dusted the sky. She let Jip out of the car.

She waited a few minutes to make certain no cars were in sight. Satisfied she and Jip were the only ones in the vicinity, she cut the rope with the penknife. She tied the two halves of the rope to Jip's leather collar, one at a time. Jip whimpered. He did not know what was happening, but he knew it was bad.

The switchback was deserted, she could see. She led Jip to the center of the road. She told him to sit there. Jip did not want to obey. She told him again to sit. This time she patted his bottom and pressed down on it to make him sit.

The ropes in her hand, she sprinted back to the shoulder to tie the end of one rope around a eucalyptus tree. Jip continued to whimper, watching her silhouette from his sitting position, the sweet musty odor of eucalyptus filling his nostrils. No matter how much he longed to be with Phyllis, he did not budge.

"Good dog," she said, returning to him. "That's a good dog."

He stood up. He wagged his tail. She patted him. She told him to sit. Grudgingly, he obeyed. She carried the end of the other rope that was tied to his collar to a eucalyptus on the opposite side of the street.

She tied the rope taut to the trunk so Jip, secured between the two trees now, could not move out of the center of the road.

Puling, Jip gazed at her with puzzlement in his doleful brown eyes.

Still no cars in view, she noticed. Good, she decided. She dashed back to her car. She could not stand to be there and watch when a car came around the switchback and met up with Jip. She had to get out of there fast before it happened. She also did not want any witnesses to see her in the area.

She jockeyed her Honda into a three-point turn. She peeled off, spewing scree on the dirt shoulder with her car's tires.

Jip howled lamentably under the starlit sky. He strained at his ropes, struggling to run after Phyllis's Honda, his collar cutting into his throat.

Phyllis felt nauseous. The blood drained from her face. She continued driving. She did not look back. Jip's death would be quick and painless. Or so she thought. She had made up her mind that it would be more humane to let Jip die now than to let him run wild in the woods and eventually starve to death or be eaten by coyotes.

Sleeping in her bed she fancied she heard a noise. She woke up. She lay still. She strained her ears. She did not hear anything. Was she dreaming? she wondered. She opened her eyes. She sat up in bed. She saw nothing. She shut her eyes. She heard the sound again. Yes! she decided. Somebody was whining. Matt?

She got out of her bed. She approached Matt's. He was fast asleep. The sound seemed to be coming from the door. A splinter of light, cast by the ceiling lamp in the corridor outside, glowed on the floor under the closed front door.

She heard the whining again. There couldn't be anyone outside the door or he would block the light glowing under it, she decided. As if reading her mind, a shadow glided across the bar of light on the door's threshold. She gasped. Frantically, she tried to figure out what to do.

She recalled her husband's revolver. She strode to the bureau at the head of her bed. She opened the bureau's bottom drawer. She snagged the revolver from under a pile of balled-up socks. Gun in hand, she stole toward the door. The whining continued.

She edged her hand toward the doorknob. She grasped the metal knob. She turned it warily, the gun in her right hand. The whining stopped. She cracked the chain-locked door an inch. She peeked out into the hall.

The hall was deserted, from what she could see through the aperture between the chain-locked door and its jamb. Her heart beat loud enough for her to hear it thumping and rattling against her ribs. Throwing caution to the wind, she shot the chain-lock and swung the door wide open. She pointed her revolver out into the hall.

Save for two cockroaches scuttling across the hall floor, she detected no movement, no life.

She wondered what to do next. She heard mumbling behind her. She felt a tug at her nightgown. She wheeled around in terror. She jerked the revolver in the direction of the tug.

"What's the matter, Mommy?" asked Matt, yawning. He rubbed his left eye with his fist.

She sighed with relief. She lowered the gun. "Nothing, dear. Go back to bed."

She picked up on him gazing at the gun in her hand. She hid the gun behind her back before he got a good look at it.

They returned to bed. Replacing the revolver in the drawer she noticed that the gun's cylinder was empty. She laughed to herself. What good was a gun without bullets? Luckily, nobody had been in the corridor.

Was it the wind that had made that horrible noise? she wondered. Then whose shadow had passed in front of the door? She decided not to think about it until tomorrow or she would never get any sleep.

She fell asleep.

She heard a harsh sound. It sounded like somebody was throwing sand against the bedroom window. Was a burglar trying to break in? she wondered. But how could anyone be outside her window? She lived on the fourth floor.

She opened her sleepy, blurry eyes. Was the curtain billowing in the dark? she wondered. Groggily, she tried to focus her eyes. A huge black bulk directly in front of her lunged through the air at her throat.

Her eyes bugged out at the growling jaws dripping saliva. Her heart stopped. She could not breathe. Her flesh crawled. She struggled to move but she could not, her body rigid. She could not even open her mouth to scream. Move! Move! she ordered her body, with no results. How long could she live with no heartbeat? she wondered.

Her heart started up again. It accelerated at a furious pace. Sweat soaked her. She managed to roll onto her side. Her heart jackhammered like it was about to burst.

She sat up. She strained her ears to hear the dog. She could hear nothing except her frantic heartbeat, which she feared would wake the neighbors on account of its deafening loudness. What if her heart burst? she wondered. She crept in the direction she thought the sound was coming from.

She would have to turn on the light. She flicked on the light switch. Nothing. The closet door opened. A black dog, its fangs bared, stood in front of her. Its brown eyes gleamed. It growled, ready to pounce. It sank its teeth into her hand, crushing her fingers between its jaws. Blood gushed out of her broken hand in red gouts.

She woke up, a scream on her lips. She blinked her eyes. She realized she still lay in bed. The closet door was closed. She glanced at her hands. Neither of them had been bitten. The apartment was quiet. Was she really awake this time or was it a dream within a dream? she wondered. Hearing a toilet flush in the bathroom above her apartment, she decided she really had woken up. She flinched as she realized her sheets were soaked in cold sweat.

"Where's Jip?" asked Matt in the morning.

"He's gone," she said.

"I didn't get a chance to say good-bye," he said, his voice breaking.

"It's better this way."

"He was my only friend."

She drove Matt to school. She returned to the apartment.

Wearing a parti-colored kerchief in her hair, she did the ironing. She heard a scratching at the door. She tiptoed toward the door, head cocked. Had Jip somehow found his way back home? she wondered. She hoped he had. She felt terrible about last night. Pangs of guilt tormented her. The thought of her leaving him in the mountains to die broke her heart. She could not believe she had done it. But she had to do it. She had no choice. There wasn't room for another mouth to feed in this family.

She twisted the doorknob a fraction at a time. She snugged her ear to the door. The scratching on the other side of the door stopped. She opened the door, wishing Jip would be there in the hall.

There was nothing in the hall. Was she going insane? she wondered. Was Jip dead or was he trying to return home?

"Jip?" she called down the corridor. "Jip?"

Nothing.

In order to find out for sure if Jip was still alive, she would have to drive up to the canyon road where she had left him last night. She bit her lower lip nervously. She did not want to go. She could not bear the sight of his dead body in the middle of the road where she had left him. What if he wasn't there? She shuddered to think. Coyotes might have dragged off his body and devoured him.

She had to know if Jip was truly dead.

She unplugged the iron. She got into her Honda compact. She fired the engine, put the car in gear, and drove to the mountain where she had left Jip.

Plagued with guilt, she found the site where she had tied Jip last night. She parked on the shoulder. She saw the ropes lying across the road. But no Jip. The ropes looked frayed to her, as though they had been run over many times by passing cars.

She climbed out of her car to inspect the area. Standing beside her car, she cast around for Jip's body. Where could he be? she wondered. She walked to the center of the road. She scrutinized the pavement. She thought she could detect a dried puddle of blood on the sun-faded blacktop. She knelt beside the stain. She examined it.

She heard a growl on the other side of the road. She jerked her head toward the sound. A black dog was standing there, glaring at her. His eyes gleamed red. Froth coated his entire mouth. His jaws hung open. Foaming saliva poured out the corners of his jowls and dripped onto the dirt beneath him.

Apprehensively, she stood up, facing him. She called to him. "Jip."

Drooling, the dog growled at her.

"Don't you recognize me?" she said.

The dog advanced toward her, his mouth foaming. A growl emanated from the bowels of his chest.

Phyllis backed away from him. She noticed he had a wound on his front leg that was bleeding. Could he have been bitten by a rabid coyote? she wondered. Jip was certainly acting strange toward her.

All of a sudden Jip charged her, growling and barking, flecks of foam shooting off his muzzle. She wasn't going to take any chances with him.

She spun around and bolted for her car. She had to get out of here. If the dog was rabid, there was no telling what he might do. She ducked into her car.

As she pulled her legs into the car, she saw Jip but a few feet away from her. She slammed the door shut in his face. He banged his head into the car door. She locked the door. She didn't know why she did, but she did. After all, how could a dog open a car door? Her imagination was working overtime. Her fears were becoming irrational, she decided.

The dog jumped up onto the door, jutted his head through the open window, and bit her arm. He clamped her arm between his jaws, drawing blood.

She screamed in pain. She hammered the dog on his snout with her other hand, trying to get him to let go of her arm. The dog shut his eyes in pain. He flinched. At that moment, Phyllis managed to pull her bloody arm free from Jip's jaws.

Jip growled. He tried to bite her arm again. She punched him in the nose. She could not roll up her window because it was automatic. She needed to turn on the ignition. She fumbled for her keys in her purse.

Jip lunged through the window to bite her throat. She recoiled away from him with mere seconds to spare. Jip was now halfway into the car. Phyllis threw her purse at his face. Jip yelped. The contents of her purse spilled out onto the floor. She spotted her car keys. She snagged them.

Leaning her body awkwardly away from Jip so she was lying in the passenger seat, she attempted to insert the key into the ignition. Her wound was racking her arm with burning pain. She had difficulty controlling her fingers. She struggled to slot the key into the ignition. He tried to bite her hand, but he could not fit his muzzle through the spokes in the steering wheel.

She slotted the key. She turned on the car's engine. She hit the window's power button. The window rose. Maddeningly slow, it seemed to her. On the verge of being trapped in the window frame by the rising window, Jip pulled his blood-spattered muzzle and trunk free of the car.

Phyllis put the car in reverse.

Jip seized the front tire in his jaws. He bit off a large chunk of rubber from it. The tire deflated. It dropped to the dirt on its steel rim. He bounded back to the rear tire. He tore a chunk of rubber out of it as well. The tire deflated.

Phyllis stepped on the gas.

The car started going in a circle, favoring its flat tires, heading toward the edge of the road behind her. Phyllis screamed.

She slammed on the brakes. She realized that if she drove any farther she would go careering off the road and down into the steep canyon below.

Turn the steering wheel, you fool! she told herself.

Jip forestalled her. He loped around to the other side of the car. He chewed a chunk of rubber out of the remaining front tire. The tire deflated. He bounded to the back of the car. He tore a hole in the last remaining inflated tire.

Phyllis tried to back up. It was useless. The tire rims were digging into the dirt and spinning without getting any purchase.

Jip slammed his growling face at her window. She started. She wondered if he could break the safety glass. He seemed to have supernatural strength. Dogs couldn't tear tires apart, could they? she wondered. And yet Jip had done it with ease.

She picked up on her cell phone in the foot well. She snagged her cell. She tried to dial 9-1-1. The cell's battery was dead. She had neglected to recharge it. Cursing, she hurled the phone to the floor.

Her wounded arm was killing her and bleeding all over her jeans. She had to stanch the bleeding. She spotted her handkerchief on the carpet, where it had fallen when she emptied out her purse. She plucked up the handkerchief and wrapped it around her bitten arm. The damn dog had not only bitten her but he had twisted his bite, ripping away a clump of her flesh in the process. He was trying to eat her alive, she realized.

She could not blame him for being hungry. Well, what did he expect? She could not afford to feed him. That was the problem in the first place. Now he was eating her. Was this some kind of revenge thing he had going? she wondered. More than likely, he was just rabid. All that froth around his muzzle and that crazy gleam in his eyes. He had to have rabies.

He lunged at her closed window again, trying to smash the glass with his paws. She had to get out of here. She gazed out the windshield. She saw that the front of the car was precariously close to the edge of the shoulder. She had to back up again.

She put the car in reverse. She applied the gas. Nothing doing, she realized. The car wasn't getting any traction with its rims spinning in the dirt. The car wasn't going anywhere. She pondered what to do next.

Suddenly the car started inching forward. She could not figure it out. She double-checked the gear shifter. It was still in reverse. Her foot was still on the brake pedal. Yet the car was moving forward, slowly but surely, of its own freewill, it seemed. The car stopped.

She breathed a sigh of relief. The car must have been sliding on its rims before, she decided. Maybe the shoulder of the road was canted downward and gravity had been pulling the car over the shoulder's lip. But still, how could the car be sliding anywhere on four flat tires?

The car was now teetering precariously on the lip of the shoulder. Phyllis decided she needed to get out of the car at once. But how? she wondered. As soon as Jip saw her open the car door, he would attack her. If she stayed in the car, it was becoming apparent she and the car would topple off the shoulder into the deep canyon below. Too, she realized her arm was still bleeding, even though it was swaddled in her handkerchief. Had Jip torn an artery in her arm? She might pass out any second from loss of blood. She needed to see a doctor.

What was that? she wondered in consternation. She felt the car shifting underneath her. It seemed to be sliding forward again. She grabbed the front seat with her hand, as though that might somehow prevent her from falling down into the coulee. What was happening?

She looked up at the rearview mirror in the middle of the windshield. She could not believe her eyes. The frigging dog had his paws on the trunk and was pushing the car forward! He was shoving her into the canyon. *Jesus Christ!* she thought with alarm. How could he push the car anywhere on four flat tires? Was he some kind of supernatural hound from hell?

She lunged toward the driver's door with its blood-splattered window. She had to get out of here. The sudden lurching of her body caused the car's front rims to slide even farther over the shoulder's dirt edge. Feeling the shifting of the car, she froze. If she tried to open the door again, she figured her movement would force the car over the edge for sure.

Now what was she going to do? she wondered. She was plumb out of ideas. She wished she had brought her gun with her, but she had no inkling at the apartment that Jip had turned into a rabid dog with superpowers and would be waiting here to assault her.

Jip barked loudly. His bark reverberated off the canyon walls. It was as if he was sounding Phyllis's death knell.

She had a sinking feeling. It reminded her of being in an elevator that was suddenly descending. Only she wasn't in an elevator. She was in her car and she was going over the cliff to the bottom of the canyon and there was nothing she could do to stop it. She screamed.

Jip stood on the dirt shoulder howling as he watched the car roll then flip over and somersault downward into an outcropping of rock a hundred-odd feet down. The car came to a halt. In a matter of seconds it burst into a corolla of unfurling black smoke and jagged yellow tongues of flames.

Jip's desolate howl echoed throughout the canyon.

The Undertaker

Dean's mortuary was going belly-up. The problem, Dean knew, was people weren't dying anymore.

What with modern technology, people lived longer than ever. Dean hated to admit it, but the new technology was bad for his business. On the other hand, Hobart's Mortuary across the street seemed to be going great guns. Dean could not figure it out.

Dean stood on the frontage of his palm-studded mortuary. Sweating in the inordinately hot humid Santa Clarita weather, he considered Hobart's Mortuary. Dean was fast approaching middle age and he didn't want to wind up old and poor in the bargain.

His assistant, Sebastian, walked up to him. "What's wrong boss?"

Without turning to face Sebastian, Dean asked, "How come Hobart's is making money hand over fist and we're going begging for customers?"

"Beats me. They got a nice spread over there. Fancy-dan green jalousies and cream-painted clapboard walls. A fanlight over their big oak door. A big sign on their emerald green grass—"

"I can see all that for myself," Dean chimed in, put out. "They look better than us because they're rolling in money."

115

"The rich get richer."

Dean eyed Sebastian's bespectacled thirtyish moon face. "You went to college, Sebastian, and got an MBA. What did you learn there?"

"That in capitalism man exploits man. And in communism, it's just the opposite."

Dean didn't laugh at the joke. In fact it graveled him. "I'm serious. If you're so smart why are you so poor?"

His face expressionless, Sebastian answered, "Because it's inevitably fated."

"Is that what they teach you in college? How to be a loser?"

Dean was fit to be tied. It wasn't just Sebastian, he knew. It was his whole damn predicament. His business was going under and he could not figure out a way to save it.

At that moment a spick-and-span copper turbo Porsche 911 drew up into the driveway of Hobart's Mortuary. Cindy Lou Hobart climbed out. Her black stretch miniskirt reached halfway up her white thighs. Catching sight of Dean out of the corner of her eye, she daintily pulled the hem of her miniskirt down.

What . . . , thought Dean, his eyes glued on her.

"There's Mrs. Hobart," said Sebastian. "She doesn't even look hot in this weather. How does she do it?" After a pause he answered his own question. "I don't think blondes sweat."

"Shut up," said Dean. "She's interested in me, if I could just turn a buck." He watched Cindy Lou enter Hobart's Mortuary then scowled as its door closed. "Hobart's is kicking our ass. They're the enemy and if we don't fight back they'll wipe the floor with us."

"How are we gonna fight back?"

Dean and Sebastian retreated to Dean's modest mortuary, Sweet Acres.

"First we'll put out the word that Hobart's runs a slimeball business," said Dean.

"How do we do that?"

Dean chewed it over for a moment before he replied, "Spread it around that he rips off gold fillings from his corpses. Stuff like that."

"I didn't know he did that."

"It doesn't matter if he does it or not," said Dean. He looked at Sebastian like he was an imbecile. "You college boys are pieces of work. What we have here is a war. Don't you get it? If we don't win anyway we can, we're gonna go under. Are you with me or do you want to surrender to Hobart?"

"I'm with you, boss. I'll do anything as long as I don't end up being a teacher."

"What's wrong with being a teacher?" Dean didn't give Sebastian a chance to answer. "Never mind. First thing we do is put up a new sign on our front lawn with a catchy slogan."

"Like what?"

"Uhhh . . . let me think . . . 'We Will Bury You.' Yeah, that's it!"

"That's great, boss. You got a mind like a steel trap."

"And I didn't go to no grad school to get it." After a beat Dean added, "We'll put up the sign so that it faces Hobart's. He can read it every day like it's his epitaph."

Sebastian nodded in admiration.

"Then we're gonna advertise on the Internet," Dean went on. "We're gonna build a Web site for Sweet Acres. The Internet's the way to go nowadays."

Sebastian nodded. "We get a domain name, then get Web hosting for our site."

Dean snapped his fingers. "I just got another idea. This'll settle Hobart's hash for sure."

"Tell me."

With both hands Dean smoothed back his greased-down black hair. "We'll spread it around that Hobart sleeps with his female cadavers."

"I'll bet he really does." Sebastian laughed.

"It's time to take the kid gloves off. We're fighting for our lives now."

Two months later business still had not picked up at Sweet Acres, whereas business was booming at Hobart's.

Dean was sitting at a table in his mortuary's deserted guest room and looking out the picture window at the long funeral procession in front of Hobart's.

"I don't get it," he told Sebastian, who was standing near the picture window.

"He's coining money like all get-out."

The sight of the funeral cortege depressed Dean. He leaned his elbows on the table in front of him. He held his head in his hands.

"I thought you put it about that he was a necrophiliac who lifted the gold fillings from his stiffs," said Dean.

"I did," said Sebastian.

Dean shook his head in disbelief. "Then why does he still have more customers than me?"

Sebastian was at a loss for words. At last he said, "The only thing I can figure is nobody believed me."

A killer headache throbbed in Dean's head. It felt like the back of his head was imploding in a pressure cooker. He could not focus his eyes.

"Business is slow," he muttered.

"Some guys have all the luck," said Sebastian as he ogled Cindy Lou prancing toward her Porsche.

Dean lifted his head from his hands. "We're gonna have to raise the stakes." He also ogled Cindy Lou.

"How?"

"We're going kaput because we aren't turning a profit. Right?"

"Right."

"We're not turning a profit because we haven't got enough customers. Right?"

"You betcha. You sound like my college prof."

"Then the only way for us to turn a profit is to either trim our overhead or increase our customers."

"But we can't trim our overhead anymore."

"That leaves us only one other option."

"But how do we increase customers?"

"I got an idea."

Sebastian looked puzzled.

"This is all-out war," said Dean.

Sebastian remained puzzled.

Soon afterwards things took a decided turn for the worse in the sleepy little California desert town of Santa Clarita.

It all began when Dean invited Joe Hobart over for dinner one night.

Hobart, the picture of a successful world-beating middle-aged businessman with his grizzled hair and grey linen bespoke suit, accepted Dean's invitation when he learned why Dean wanted to see him.

Dean sat at his dinner table. Cindy Lou and Hobart sat across from him.

"Yes," said Dean. "I'm thinking about selling out to you, Joe. You've been pestering me from day one to do it."

"I'm glad to hear you've finally come to your senses," said Hobart, all smiles. "Everybody wins if you sell out to me. You'll see, Dean." Hobart twirled his fork in his vermicelli. He inserted a wad of the spaghetti into his mouth. Finished chewing, he added, "I like this spaghetti sauce. I've never tasted anything quite like it."

"Beside everything else, Sebastian is a great cook."

"It's my mother's recipe," said Sebastian, sitting at the other end of the table. He looked grateful for the compliment. "She's Italian."

"We never had a chance up against you," Dean told Hobart. "How can the little fish win against the big fish?"

"Well, David had his slingshot," chipped in Cindy Lou. She was wearing a low-cut shocking pink blouse to draw attention to her cleavage.

"Yep," said Dean, "and that was the end of Goliath."

"I don't know where this is leading us," said Hobart, his patience wearing thin. "Let's get down to brass tacks. How much do you want, Dean?" Hobart belched. He screwed up his face in discomfort for a second.

"Are you OK, honey?" asked Cindy Lou.

"Yeah. Must be something I ate," Hobart joked.

Cindy Lou took stock of the dining room in disgust. "It's probably this shabby dining room making you sick."

Dean could not help but wince at her cut. Women could be so cruel, he knew. Cindy Lou was young and beautiful but nasty to boot.

"How can you stand eating in this dump night after night, Dean?" she asked.

"Cindy Lou is the editor of a fashion magazine," explained Hobart. "She knows whereof she speaks."

Dean could not think of anything to say. He felt humiliated. But he would have his revenge, he knew . . . all in due time.

Cindy Lou took in Hobart's face with alarm. "You look pale, honey. Do you need fresh air? It's this awful place."

Dean continued to put a lid on his anger as Cindy Lou kept spewing her callous remarks about his residence. He would not allow her to get under his skin. After all, he wanted them to finish their supper.

"You never had a chance against me," Hobart told Dean. "I'm a good businessman."

"You're also rich," said Dean.

"Because I'm a good businessman."

"And because you have well-fixed parents," Dean said under his breath.

"What?"

"Nothing." Dean smiled.

Hobart raised his voice. "Come on. Let's talk turkey. How much do you want?"

He shoveled more vermicelli into his mouth. The thin strands seemed to wriggle and crawl up his lantern jaw like white worms.

"How much do you think my mortuary is worth?" asked Dean.

"Not much." Hobart grinned at his joke. Then he looked sick to his stomach. He hunched over his plate for a few seconds before he managed to sit up.

"We better leave," said Cindy Lou, taking in Hobart's distress.

"Not till I buy him out," said Hobart.

Before his last word had left his mouth Hobart's eyes bugged out of his head. His face turned livid. He clutched his throat as if strangling himself. He attempted to leap to his feet only to tangle his legs under the tabletop and fall with a crash into his plate of vermicelli.

Cindy Lou sprang to her feet. A scream caught in her throat.

"I've changed my mind," said Dean. I'm not gonna sell."

Cindy Lou felt for a pulse in Hobart's neck. Nonplussed, she shook her head.

"It must've been a heart attack," said Sebastian.

"I'll be glad to bury him here," Dean told Cindy Lou.

"What am I gonna do?" she said. She had become unglued. Her blue eyes gaped at Dean. "I don't know anything about running a mortuary."

Dean got up from his chair and stood beside her. "What about becoming my partner?"

He put his arm around her wasp waist to comfort her. He had never laid eyes on such a narrow waist. It was the most exciting aspect of her hourglass figure, Dean decided.

"I-I-I," she stammered. "I've always liked you, Dean." She looked up into his face. "Those big grey eyes of yours."

"And I've always liked your pair of big, round, blue eyes." But he wasn't exactly looking at her eyes at that instant.

"The problem is," she said and pulled away from him, "you're too poor." She paused a beat. "You are asking for my hand, aren't you?"

"Yes," he croaked, his mouth dry.

"I can't marry beneath me. You understand."

The tease! thought Dean. "Who's gonna run your mortuary?"

"I guess I'll have to. Unless you can start turning a profit at this—this—" she gestured with a wince of disdain for Dean's mortuary—"this whatever." She made for the front door.

"Let me bury Joe. It's the least I can do for you."

"No. I'll do it myself," she said.

She strutted out the door without looking back.

"Your plan seems to have backfired," Sebastian told Dean.

"I'm not dead yet," Dean grumbled. "I knew she was greedy but not *that* greedy."

"Where are you gonna get the kind of money to please the likes of her?"

Dean patted Sebastian's back. "This is only the beginning. You'll see."

The town's population shrank at an alarming rate after Hobart's demise. Business picked up proportionately at Sweet Acres, as many of the heart attacks that caused the spate of recent deaths occurred at Dean's dinner table or a short while after the victim dined at Dean's.

When Dean ran out of customers all he had to say to Sebastian was, "Business is slow," and

Sebastian would cook up a spaghetti dinner. Dean would invite guests over to enjoy Sebastian's special tomato sauce. And business would pick up afterwards.

Dean became so prosperous at the sudden passing away of the townspeople that his business eventually rivaled Hobart's. Dean had to hire construction workers to add annexes to his mortuary so that it became bigger than Hobart's—and fancier with a marble staircase inside it.

When Cindy Lou set her eyes on Dean's magnificent mortuary she agreed to marry him and let him co-opt Hobart's.

While Dean prospered, however, the townsfolk worried at the unexplained increase in deaths in Santa Clarita. They fretted that a plague was decimating their numbers. Fearing AIDS or a contagious disease like it, scores of Claritites migrated elsewhere.

The city set to going broke. Nobody was left to pay taxes. The mayor declared there was no plague and urged Claritites to stay put in Santa Clarita or the city would cease to exist.

Business started dropping off a tad for Dean, too. People became apprehensive of eating at his house because of all the heart attacks that occurred after guests dined there. However, they could not get enough of his fancy digs. They started calling it a palazzo and many of them accepted his dinner invitations just so they could eyeball it.

Hobart's twentysomething daughter from a prior marriage, Lucinda was an aspiring actress. Already suspicious of foul play in her father's death, she became even more so when she saw how wealthy Dean was becoming. She never liked Dean in the first place. After he married her stepmother

Cindy Lou, Lucinda downright hated Dean. The whole setup smelled fishy to her.

She contacted Sheriff Fuegel and made him aware of her suspicions regarding her father's untimely death. She asked him to exhume Hobart's corpse and have an autopsy performed on it.

"Why?" asked the potbellied Fuegel in his office.

He held a bag of Cheetos in one hand and a Styrofoam cup of piping hot coffee in the other. Orange crumbs from the Cheetos stuck to his bushy mustache.

"Because Daddy was healthy as an ox. I can't believe he had a heart attack."

"That's what the doctor said."

"Did he perform an autopsy?"

"No. There was no call to."

"There. You see. Then how can you be sure he died of a heart attack?"

"Do you have a good reason to suspect foul play?" The sheriff cleared his throat. He was having trouble speaking because of a Cheeto particle wedged in the back of his throat.

"Yes! Why do you think I want you to perform an autopsy?"

"Calm down, will you? Who would want to kill your dad?"

"Dean."

"Dean who?"

"Dean King." Lucinda wondered if the sheriff was as dense as he acted.

"The undertaker who married your mom?" The sheriff's plump face registered surprise. His bushy eyebrows like caterpillars rose up his forehead.

"That's why he wanted my dad dead. So he could marry her. Isn't it obvious?" she said in exasperation.

The sheriff thought Lucinda was even better looking than her stepmother, what with her blonde ponytail and cute pink face. That being said, he didn't put any stock in Lucinda's accusations. He sighed. He massaged his forehead.

"I'll look into it," he said wearily.

"I'm going to Dean's house to have dinner with him tomorrow night to see if I can find out what's really going on there."

Her face set with determination, Lucinda bustled out of the sheriff's office.

Meanwhile spectators came from miles around to gawk at Dean's palatial mortuary. It was the talk of the town. Half the time it was swarming with shiny black hearses and funeral cavalcades. The pick of the litter was Dean's pride and joy, his 24 karat gold-plated stretch hearse.

The night after Lucinda went to the sheriff, Dean told Sebastian at Sweet Acres, "Business is slow."

Sebastian proceeded to whip up a batch of home-cooked spaghetti for Lucinda, Dean, and Cindy Lou.

At the dinner table when Sebastian offered Lucinda her plate of spaghetti she put up her nose and said, "I don't like spaghetti."

Sebastian looked daggers at her, but not for long. The expression on his face soon morphed into one of sweetness. "You've obviously never tasted my special sauce. One taste of it will put you in heaven."

"I think not," said Lucinda and pushed the plate away from her.

Sebastian glowered at her.

"That's OK," Dean told him. "Fix her whatever she wants."

"I eat only raw vegetables," said Lucinda.

"She's a vegan," said Cindy Lou. "She picked it up at college."

"My spaghetti doesn't have meat in it," protested Sebastian.

"The meat's in the sauce," said Lucinda. "I might eat spaghetti with no sauce on it and no butter."

"What kind of spaghetti is that?"

Sebastian set the steaming dish of spaghetti in front of her.

Grimacing, Lucinda waved her hands at it. "Take it away."

"You don't know good food when you see it. Smell that delicious aroma."

"I won't eat it!"

"Take it away," said Dean. "She doesn't know what she's missing." He scarfed down a mouthful of spaghetti and licked the sauce off his lips with a smile.

"The sheriff phoned us and told me you want him to exhume Joe's corpse," Cindy Lou told Lucinda. "Is that true?"

"Yeah."

"You should've asked me before going to the sheriff. He needs my permission for an autopsy."

"Then give it."

"Why should I?"

Lucinda hung fire for a few moments, unsure of how much to tell her stepmother. Lucinda decided to tell her everything. "Because someone might've killed him."

Dean chewed his spaghetti. He watched Lucinda without expression.

"I don't think an autopsy's a good idea." It was Sebastian who spoke. "That's desecration of the dead."

Dean continued munching away, lost in his food, his face blank.

"I don't know," said Cindy Lou. "If it'll set Lucinda's mind at ease, maybe it's the right thing to do. Maybe . . ." Her voice trailed off.

Sebastian shook his head vehemently. "It's desecration."

"We have to find out the truth," demanded Lucinda.

"That we should," said Cindy Lou.

Sebastian made to grab Lucinda's ponytail then thought better of it. He gained control of himself in the nick of time without her noticing his attempt.

"What do you think, honey?" Cindy Lou asked Dean.

With a paper napkin Dean wiped spaghetti sauce off the corners of his mouth. "Maybe it's for the best."

Lucinda could not believe her ears. She thought for sure Dean would object to an autopsy.

Equally puzzled by Dean's acquiescence to Lucinda's request, Sebastian exchanged glances with Dean.

"Yes," said Cindy Lou.

Sebastian approached Dean and whispered through his teeth, "If you're setting me up as your fall guy, I'll blow the whistle on you. I'm digging him up tonight so nobody's gonna find anything in his grave."

Later that night Sebastian crept alone into the Sweet Acres cemetery. Lantern in one hand, a spade in the other, he located Hobart's grave. Distrusting Dean he was also packing a gun. A warm humid wind was blowing in from the west. Save for the soughing of the wind, there was no other sound. There was no moon that he could see.

He thought it was a major accomplishment by Dean to have persuaded Cindy Lou to disinter her husband from Hobart's cemetery and transfer the corpse over to Sweet Acres, where it lay now. It certainly made Sebastian's task a lot easier. He didn't have as far to walk. The cadaver was in his backyard, so to speak.

Sebastian set the lantern down at the edge of the grave. He commenced to exhume Hobart, wishing the shovel would not make such a god-awful racket as it clanged against rocks and pebbles in the dirt. He kept looking up apprehensively, suspecting somebody would hear the cacophony and come out and inspect the cemetery.

Sebastian sweated in the muggy air. He stood rooted to the spot when he heart fluttering overhead. Some night bird, he decided, and resumed digging. An hour later he had dug only two feet into the grave. He was getting nowhere fast. His shirt was wringing with sweat. At this rate he would be shoveling all night.

There was nothing for it but to continue. He could not allow an autopsy on Hobart's corpse. The medical examiner might find traces of the cyanide in Hobart's system.

Gasping with exhaustion, Sebastian manhandled the shovel. He was so rapt in concentration that he almost didn't hear a voice say, "Drop that shovel and climb out of there."

Sebastian glanced toward the direction of the voice but could not make out the man who spoke. The man was standing behind the lantern in the shadows out of the light it was shedding on the grave.

"Who's there?" asked Sebastian. "That you, Dean?"

"Sheriff Fuegel. Now get out of there!"

Sebastian could make out the sheriff's bulky dark silhouette behind the lantern. In one fell swoop Sebastian dropped his spade, withdrew the 9 mm automatic from his waistband, and turned the barrel on the sheriff.

Before Sebastian had time to pull the trigger the sheriff pumped three .38 rounds into Sebastian's chest, ripping Sebastian's lungs and heart apart.

"Why'd you have to go and do that?" grumbled the sheriff.

The next day the medical examiner performed an autopsy on Hobart's cadaver. The sheriff visited Dean at Sweet Acres. In the guest room he told Dean the results.

"Hobart died of cyanide poisoning," said the sheriff. "The poison's effects mimic a heart attack in the victim." He fingered his flaxen mustache, trying to wipe nicotine stains off its lower edge as he picked up on his face's reflection in the cheval glass.

Dean wondered why Fuegel even bothered. Fuegel wasn't the handsomest man he had ever seen—not by a long shot, noted Dean.

"Somebody poisoned him. Is that what you're saying?" asked Dean.

"Sure as shooting. And it's dead-bang certain your assistant Sebastian did it."

"I can't believe it."

"Why else would he be digging up Hobart's stiff in the middle of the night unless he wanted to rob the grave so we couldn't do an autopsy on Hobart?"

"What's Sebastian got to say about this?"

"Nothing. He ended up like Hobart."

Dean blinked in amazement. He said nothing.

"I didn't want to shoot him but he pulled a gun on me," the sheriff went on. "Lucky you heard him out there digging and phoned me or he might've got away with robbing the grave."

"I didn't know it was Sebastian doing the digging. I just heard a ruckus someone was making in the cemetery." Dean shambled toward the picture window. "This is all hard to believe."

"The only thing I can't figure out is motive. Why did Sebastian have it in for Hobart?" The sheriff scratched his thinning chestnut hair. He turned to leave.

"Thanks for dropping by, Sheriff."

The sheriff met Lucinda in the driveway and told her about Sebastian and the cyanide.

"So you were right after all—about foul play, I mean," added the sheriff.

Frowning, Lucinda shook her head. "I can't believe it was Sebastian who killed Dad. Are you sure it wasn't Dean?"

"Couldn't've been. In fact it was Dean who called me to let me know Sebastian was robbing Hobart's grave."

Business dropped off at Sweet Acres after Sebastian's death. Word got around that he had been poisoning the dinner guests at the mortuary. Sweet Acres was now in the grips of a recession. Like in the bad old days, Dean realized, people weren't kicking the bucket anymore.

Cindy Lou complained to Dean at every turn.

"If you don't buy me a new cabochon diamond necklace, I'm gonna divorce you," she told him one week when not a single person bought the farm.

Dean took up cooking spaghetti dinners a la Sebastian.

On a sudden, business ramped up threefold. It looked like the recession at Sweet Acres was a thing of the past. The corpses kept rolling in. Coffins jammed the guest room and flooded into the aisles. The cadavers' waxen faces reminded Dean of cabochon diamonds.

The townsfolk were dropping like flies. Once again, publicly the mayor declared there was no plague. Privately, he feared the plague had returned to lay waste to Santa Clarita. It didn't matter what the mayor said. The townsfolk didn't listen to him. They could see for their own eyes what has happening to their friends and neighbors.

As his business thrived Dean celebrated by buying Cindy Lou a new cabochon diamond necklace.

For Dean the problem was, what would he do when there weren't any more corpses? Santa Clarita was practically a ghost town already, what with so many deaths and the throngs of citizens who were moving out.

Dean could see but one solution: expand his business to another city. As Sebastian had once explained to him, in capitalism a business enterprise must continue to find new markets, i.e., continue to expand, in order for it to turn more profits.

Sebastian was a bright kid when it came to school learning, decided Dean, but he was a downright doofus when it came to human nature. That was the trouble with college kids. No street smarts. Couldn't Sebastian foresee that Dean was going to sell him out for Cindy Lou's sake?

As the bodies piled up in Dean's mortuary, Lucinda became more and more suspicious of Dean. She was convinced he had poisoned her father or had ordered Sebastian to do his dirty work for him.

She wondered why Dean had not poisoned her. It was obvious to her that he despised her. She remembered she had refused to eat Sebastian's spaghetti and now refused to eat Dean's. That got her to thinking. Could the poison be in the spaghetti sauce?

One day she stole into Dean's deserted kitchen. She rooted through the spices on the spice rack. The trouble was she had no idea what cyanide looked or smelled like. She would need a chemist to examine these spices and detect cyanide.

As she was opening the cruet of oregano, Dean walked into the kitchen. Seeing what she was doing he grabbed a butcher knife from the tabletop. He lunged at her, knife in hand. She dodged his blow. Terrified, she cut and ran.

When she bucketed onto the driveway, she glanced over her shoulder to see if Dean was pursuing her. She didn't spot him. She figured he didn't want the neighbors to see him chasing her with a butcher knife in his hand.

She spent the rest of the day hiding in town, planning her next move.

At last she returned to Sweet Acres for dinner, apprehensive but dogged.

Before she entered the dining room she set a fire inside a wastebasket in the hallway that skirted the dining room.

She strolled into the dining room, trying her best to look nonchalant. She saw that dinner was already served. Dean, Cindy Lou, and the sheriff were all seated at the table.

"I'm sorry I'm late," Lucinda said.

She glanced fearfully at Dean, who seemed to show no interest in her. She had no intention of telling the inept sheriff about Dean's assault on her. She was going to take this into her own hands. Sniffing smoke she whirled toward the hallway.

"Fire!" she screamed.

Smoke billowed into the dining room.

Dean, Cindy Lou, and the sheriff bolted from their seats. They dashed toward the hall. Lucinda bounded equally as fast to the dinner table. She switched Dean's plate of spaghetti with the sheriff's.

Dean and the sheriff extinguished the fire in short order, using a miniature fire extinguisher mounted near the front door for just such an occasion. They returned to the dining room with Cindy Lou in tow. Grimacing, she was fanning her face to clear the smoke away from her nose and eyes.

In consternation Lucinda watched the sheriff sit down in Dean's chair. She didn't know what to do. She was on the verge of yelling at the sheriff not to sit there.

While she looked on, Dean stared hard at the sheriff. Realizing his gaffe the sheriff got up and sat in his own seat. A broad smile on his face, Dean sat in his. He commenced eating his spaghetti.

Lucinda sighed with relief.

"We'll be moving to greener pastures next week, Sheriff," announced Dean between bites.

Fuegel looked surprised. "Is that so? Why is that?"

"To expand our business. To find new territory."

Watching Dean chomp his spaghetti, Lucinda knew better.

Instead of finding new territory the next day, Cindy Lou would be finding a new husband.

Shambles

Each day was like the next, ad infinitum ad nauseam. To put it bluntly, I was in a rut. I could not put my finger on the exact cause for my gloomy disposition. A crushing feeling of dissatisfaction and angst weighed upon me. Each morning, I had to hypnotize myself to go to a wage-slave job that I didn't care for.

It got so I could not tell one day from the other.

"We've got some June gloom on tap today in So. Cal.," droned the radio announcer I was listening to as I drove to work.

It was like I was standing outside myself watching this person, me, go to work like a wind-up toy without a mind. I began to think I was going insane.

And I'm telling myself all along that I can't control what happens to me. I can only control how I react to it. But, for some reason, my stoicism is not satisfactory. I feel like I'm rationalizing a life which in reality is a dead end. It's like I'm seeing my reflection in a million mirrors, and my reflection never changes till I die. This revelation about my future disquiets me no end.

I'm clueless about the image that I'm projecting at work. I have no idea how my coworkers see me. To be honest, I don't care. All I know is that it's not me but a character, a robot, more precisely, invented by my supervisors and by my complicity with their invention.

But there's another me, which they don't know about. It's the me standing outside of their invention of me, watching him (i.e., their concept of me). There's a killer inside this other me, watching.

I parked my pickup in the company parking lot. I lumbered out of the front seat. The radio announcer was right, I realized, about the weather. It was overcast. I walked into the warehouse. I punched in at the time clock.

"What's up?" asked Dan, one of my coworkers at the delivery company.

"Nothing."

He handed me a two-foot-tall card with signatures scribbled on it. "Valerie's leaving our company for another."

"I can't imagine why."

"Very funny, Mark. All joking aside, do you want to sign our card and make a donation to her?"

He showed me a number ten envelope with bills stuffed inside it. He opened the envelope for me to take a gander at the cash.

"Why does she need a donation if she's already got another job?" I asked.

"Come on. It's the right thing to do."

"Who is Valerie?"

My answer annoyed him. He shook his equine head. He reminded me of Mr. Ed, that white horse on the eponymous sixties' TV series. He even sounded sort of like Mr. Ed with his deep voice.

"Duh, she works here," he said.

"I don't remember her."

"She still works here, so far."

"I still don't remember her."

"The weight-challenged girl with the red hair."

"Weight-challenged? Run that by me again, Dan."

"You heard me."

"You've been working here too long. I can't understand you."

"I can't be any clearer."

Dan's political correctness irked me. "Are you trying to say she's fat?"

"I'm not trying to say that. I said exactly what I meant."

"That's the point. What *do* you mean?"

He sighed. His horse nostrils flared. Then he asked politely, "Do you want to donate or not?"

"Not."

"No problem."

Card in hand, he strutted away from me and approached a nearby worker.

I knew Dan was a projection. At what precise moment I knew it, I can't tell. He was supervisor Andy's projection of the polite, concerned worker.

He was like all the workers here, walking around in their yellow uniforms, having no concept of who they were. They had no inkling that they had been co-opted by Andy, created by Andy, and ultimately inhabited by Andy. Andy was pulling their strings.

I snuck outside the warehouse into the parking lot to get some air. We were half a mile from Will Rogers State Beach. It was a few minutes after eight.

Onshore beach fog hovered and gyred overhead. I took a deep breath. I could smell the fragrant aroma of salty sea, which, borne on the fog, clung to my lungs. It refreshed me like a piquant food. It was even better than food, though, because it was a natural scent, a life-full scent, if you will. I wanted to swirl it around in my lungs, the brackish mist, to taste every morsel of it, to taste the woman's-nipple bitterness of it, to absorb it in my being—

And then it was spoiled, just like that. By the sweet greasy stink of frying fat emanating from a roach coach that said *Mariscos* on its sides. The Mexican food truck was parked near the curb and was dripping hot cooking grease on the asphalt. The whole truck seemed to glisten with grease.

It wasn't the same for me after that.

For a while, I watched the day laborers constellate around the *Mariscos* truck. They held hot smoking food in their hands. Tacos, burritos, quesadillas, fajitas. They devoured their food with relish. Then I watched the gulls wheeling overhead slicing through the fog banks. The gulls glided through the fog, in and out of sight effortlessly, cawing with hunger.

I figured the gulls were attracted by the sweet greasy odor emitted by the food truck.

I could not get that cloying fat smell out of my lungs no matter how hard I tried to replace it with that of the bracing sea fog. Disappointed, I entered the warehouse.

Tony Peece the Indian was waiting for me inside. He had a ring in his nose. He had a ring in his ear. The front of his head was shaved bald. The back of his head sported black ropy hair that fell to his shoulders. He stood five feet eight with his shoes on.

"Having fun?" he asked.

"How did you know?"

How did he know I had a gun? Guns were illegal at our company. Possession of them was grounds, in fact, for instant dismissal. If Chainsaw Andy found out about my gun, he would fire me on the spot. No questions asked. I would not even have the right to file a grievance with the union to contest my termination.

I had a Beretta .380 automatic stashed in my locker upstairs. I would need the piece to free myself from servitude. What puzzled me was how Peece had tumbled to my gun. I had told no one about it.

"It wasn't me," said Peece.

"What?"

"Don't look so pissed off. It's only a job." He smiled.

I said nothing. I was looking at the green tattoos up and down the length of his arm. Actually, tattoos graced both of his arms. He was the resident illustrated man. Most of the tattoos didn't look recognizable. I did manage, however, to recognize green tears on his forearms.

"Don't you like your job?" he asked.

"No."

"That's not the right answer."

"Which is . . . ?"

"Fuck you, of course."

"Oh."

"Or, I want to clock a skinhead."

Whatever that meant. I didn't see the connection.

Like Dan, Peece was Chainsaw Andy's projection. He was the Indian with a chip on his shoulder. Peece had done time in the navy and in the joint before working here. For his money, he had a right to be resentful.

Now he lived in Orange County, not so much because he wanted to live there but because his neighbors didn't want him to live there. That may sound like an oxymoron. It wasn't. Peece didn't do things because he wanted to. He did them because other people didn't want him to. He thrived on conflict. It was what he lived for.

Peece nudged my arm with his thick elbow. "I broke a skinhead's nose the other day at a restaurant in Venice. The dip gave me a *sieg heil* salute and thought he'd get away with it." He offered me a toothy grin.

I got the impression that he was trying to tell me something. The question was, what? Was he insinuating that I was a skinhead and had better watch my back when I was around him? Why? I didn't shave my head. Had he brought up the matter of my gun and the skinhead story to goad me? I felt a disconnect between us.

"What are you trying to tell me?" I asked.

"I'm not *trying* to tell you anything. I did tell it to you. Do I have to spell it out?"

"If you don't mind."

"You're unbelievable, Mark. Think vacation, guy."

He left me.

I piled crates onto a dolly. I wheeled it out to the loading dock. One of the dolly's tires needed air. As a result, I felt the dolly lugging to my right as I pushed it. I had difficulty controlling it.

I wondered if any of my coworkers knew, like I did, that they were Andy's projections. Was anyone else willing to kill to be free? The tree of freedom had to be watered with blood from time to time. Didn't Jefferson say that?

"Wasting time again, Banyon? You loser."

It was Albert, not Andy, who was addressing me. Albert was standing on the loading dock lording it over two workers that were loading a big rig backed up against the dock. The two were using a forklift to raise packages on wooden pallets and deposit them into the rear of the truck.

Albert was Andy's protégé. Albert tried his damnedest to treat people even worse than did Andy. Try though he might to sound tough, Albert came off sounding like a comedian or a two-fisted pixie at best.

He swaggered around the station with his fists balled, his teeth bared. He leaned back as he talked to workers, his arms out at his sides, his face tilted upward, like he was going to fall on his butt any second on account of the strain of puffing out his chest and arching his spine backwards.

In a nutshell, the jug-eared middle-aged Albert was a scab-picking hate monger. Nobody liked him. Apparently, nobody had ever liked him. As a result, he went out of his way to make all the workers miserable by leaving no stone unturned and watching with glee what crawled out.

Nobody respected him, so he made sure to disrespect everyone.

One of his favorite lines was, "Is there anyone I haven't insulted?" Then he would break out into sadistic laughter.

"You're the worst loser Andy ever hired, Banyon," he told me now, as I was rolling the dolly onto the dock.

"Tell me what you really think, Albert."

What could only be characterized as a shit-eating grin cracked his face. "You're an incompetent bum."

I could not believe my ears. Even Albert knew I had a gun. How did he know it was an incompetent gun? Had he test-fired it? Confiscated it? For that matter, was it still in my locker?

Did Albert know he was Andy's projection of a shitheel loser, a bureaucratic climber manqué of the worst order?

"Do you think I like this job?" I asked rhetorically.

"You're not allowed to say that," said Albert, anticipating my negative response to my question.

"Even if it's true?"

"Especially if it's true."

"I don't understand."

"Chainsaw Andy doesn't like that kind of talk. It signifies low morale, the morale of a loser like you, Banyon. He's fired people for less. Hence his nickname, as I'm sure you're aware."

"You want a cover-up. Is that what you're saying?"

"I'm saying you know where the door is if you don't like it here."

"But I don't know where the money is if I leave."

"So shut up. Or I'll tell asshole Andy about you." He put on a pair of Ray-Ban shades even though it was overcast outside.

"He wouldn't like hearing that you called him that."

Albert thrust his clean-shaven chin at me. "He's not gonna hear it from me. Or from you."

"What are you trying to say to me?"

It was difficult to understand anyone at this company. Andy's projections were becoming increasingly incomprehensible. I wondered how they could exist outside of his organization. How could they exist with their families or friends? How could they even buy groceries at the supermarket?

Albert was the lowest kind of fawning bootlicker. He was either under your heel or at your throat, as Churchill once said of the Nazis. It would scare the living daylights out of Albert if he believed I would tell Andy what Albert had just called him.

"I'm telling you you're a bum," said Albert. "Which part of *bum* don't you understand?"

He was telling me to get my gun. He was telling me that that was my only alternative if I didn't want to be co-opted by Andy and turned into nothing more than a projection by him, like Andy had done to the other workers.

In my case, Andy's projection of me was not complete. He had transformed most of me into a quiet, biddable worker. However, unlike my fellow coworkers, I could stand outside of myself and see what was happening. I could see what Andy was trying to do to us. There was one more difference between me and the other workers. Unlike them, I had the killer inside me.

"Did you hear me?" Albert asked.

"Yeah."

"Did you understand me?"

"Not clearly."

"What's taking so long?"

I paused a beat. "Your obfuscation."

The blood drained from his face. When people used words he didn't know around him, it ticked him off. "My what?"

"Never mind. I need the money."

Albert scoffed. "Then get back to work!"

To become one of Andy's projections was the last thing I wanted. To escape this prison of automatons I needed money. My exit out of here ran straight through Andy's office because his office contained his vault.

I walked upstairs to the locker room. I wondered if my gun would be in my locker. It was open to question, considering the fact that everybody and his mother seemed to know that I had a gun.

With some trepidation I dialed the combination lock. I clicked open the lock. I opened my locker door.

Under a heap of old clothes I found the Beretta right where I had secreted it.

I had the .380 automatic inside my rear waistband in a matter of seconds, underneath my company Windbreaker. I made a beeline for Andy's office.

"Where are you going?" Albert challenged me.

My mind worked overtime to manufacture a lie. I could not come up with one. I told the truth. "To Andy's office."

"Am I harassing you?" He leered at me.

I said nothing. I knew he was trying to provoke me.

"Why are you going to his office?" he asked.

He was probably scared I was going to tell Andy that he had called Andy an asshole.

"He wants to see me," I said.

"Get a move on it," Albert cut in.

Inside Andy's capacious dim-lit office, a projector was beaming a movie on a wide screen. His back to me, Andy was sitting behind the projector. I could not discern his features. I didn't recognize the movie. I didn't really care.

Andy had a pocket garden underneath the bay window in his office. This was only the second time I had ever been in his office. Most of the plants in the garden seemed to be philodendrons and snake plants. Those were the only plants I could identify anyway.

I focused my mind on the matter at hand. I had come here for the company safe. I knew where it was—to the left of the movie screen, in the back of the office.

I locked the office door behind me.

There was nothing surprising about the movie until I saw myself appear in it. Andy had filmed me on the loading dock one day. The control freak was projecting my image on his screen at that very moment. Trying to capture me there? Trying to complete my transformation into one of his projections?

I had no idea. I didn't want to find out. I had to act fast. I had to steal my own life back from him.

A loud crash in an adjoining room to my right startled me. I whirled to check out the source of the commotion. I forgot about Andy for the moment.

There was a ruckus going on behind a door that led to a communicating room.

I stole toward the door.

The projector continued humming as it threw my image walking around the workroom floor on the movie screen.

As I approached the door I heard a spate of banging and thumping emanating from the adjoining room. Somebody groaned.

Gun in hand, I tried the doorknob. It gave. I twisted it charily. I wasn't sure I wanted to enter the room. I just wanted to know what was creating such a racket. The cacophony beyond the door continued unabated. I cracked the door. I peeked inside.

It was a scene of rank mayhem that greeted my eyes. Chairs and desks were overturned helter-skelter as though a tornado had touched down on them.

At last I saw the reason for the tumult as I opened the door farther. I could not believe my gaping eyes. I stood transfixed, aghast at the sight. Albert was in the process of tearing one of Peece's arms off. Peece screamed in agony as he saw his arm literally ripped out of his shoulder. His face blanched. I thought he might pass out. A fountain of blood spewed from the remaining stump of his amputated arm.

My mind struggled to comprehend the grisly spectacle that was taking place before me. I saw Albert raise the arm to his mouth. He took a huge bite out of the arm's bicep. He began chewing the muscle. Blood smeared his face, dripping from his lips.

Then Albert took the arm and swatted Peece's head with it. Peece screamed in outrage as well as in pain. He attempted to take a swing at Albert with his remaining arm. Albert snagged the arm. He tore it, too, out of its socket.

Peece roared in agony. Blood was now gushing out of both of his arm sockets, sluicing the overturned furniture as well as the carpet.

I could not make out Albert's face. He was turned away form me as he assaulted Peece. Albert was now munching on Peece's other arm like it was a drumstick. The crunching sounds Albert's teeth were making against bone and flesh were sickening to hear.

I could not stand it any longer. Albert had obviously gone berserk. I told him to stop or I'd shoot him.

He ignored me. He kept devouring Peece's arms. Bleeding copiously, Peece watched Albert in a daze. Peece looked like he would black out any second. I could not believe that Peece was still conscious considering the amount of blood he had already lost.

I yelled at Albert again to stop. No response. Enough was enough. I was nauseated by this scene from a slaughterhouse. I trained my pistol on Albert. I shot him twice in the back. Nothing. I shook my head in bafflement. I glanced at my automatic. My bullets had no effect on Albert. I shot him again.

He ignored me. He kept feasting on Peece's arms, savoring their flesh. From shock and loss of blood, Peece fainted.

I shot Albert again. This time I got his attention. He whirled around to confront me. I didn't recognize him. I recognized him from the back, it was true, but from the front it was a different story. His face had undergone a hideous transformation. It was partially decomposed. Bits of his skull were exposed through his tattered, scrofulous skin. It was the face of a long-dead corpse.

He growled at me. He flung one of Peece's arms at my head. The arm sailed through the air, dripping blood. I ducked. Blood splattered the ceiling and stippled the wall beside me.

Out of the corner of my eye, I picked up on movement behind Albert. Albert must have heard the scuffling associated with the movement. He turned around to investigate. It was Dan.

Dan was charging Albert. Dan let loose a banshee yell as he lunged in a blind fury at Albert. Albert clubbed Dan in the head with Peece's other arm.

Dan reeled from the blow. His movements jerky and stiff, Albert lurched after Dan. Albert seemed spastic, like he lacked complete control of his limbs.

Dan grabbed a laptop off a nearby desk. He hurled the laptop at Albert's head. The laptop smashed into Albert's blood-soaked ghoulish face. Albert shook his head, trying to recover from the blow, trying to come to his senses. The laptop crashed to the floor.

Albert staggered inexorably toward Dan. Dan didn't know what to do. He snagged another laptop off a desktop. He cast the laptop at Albert.

Albert batted it away. The deflected laptop caromed into the window next to him, shattering the pane. Shards of glass showered onto the carpet.

Albert lunged at Dan, grabbed Dan's hand, and wrenched Dan's arm from its socket. Blood jetted all over the room, drenching everything in sight.

Albert chomped on Dan's arm. Seeing his detached arm clamped in Albert's mouth, Dan let out a bloodcurdling scream. In shock, Dan collapsed to the floor unconscious.

I didn't know what to do. I had to put an end to this madness. My bullets had no effect on Albert, it was plain to see. What else could I do?

Albert advanced on Dan's sprawled, motionless body. Growling, Albert clutched Dan's leg and tugged on it. Dan's leg separated from his hip. Blood from the femoral artery flooded the carpet.

Albert stuck Dan's foot in his mouth. Albert spat out Dan's Reebok track shoe and clamped down with his jaws on Dan's foot, sock and all. Albert masticated the foot bones, sock, and flesh. He moaned with what sounded like pleasure.

A stark sensation of disgust mixed with horror overwhelmed me. I decided I had no time to lose. Once Albert finished cannibalizing Dan, he would inevitably add me to his feast.

I stalked up to Albert, who was facing away from me. He was crouching on the rug, rapt in his meal. I took aim, but not at his back this time. At point-blank range, I shot Albert in the head.

Albert's head jerked forward. Most of his wasted face and clumps of spongy grey matter blew out of Albert's head across Dan's lifeless body in a mixture of bloody spray and chunks. This time my bullet had hit pay dirt. Albert slumped to the floor.

Apprehensively, I watched his lifeless body to see if he would get up. I wasn't positive my .380 Beretta had done the trick. How could I be sure of anything after I had plugged Albert in the back earlier with four rounds that had not even slowed him down?

Gun in hand, I stood there watching Albert for the better part of two minutes. Albert did not budge. Satisfied, I retreated from his corpse.

I made for the door to Andy's office, bound and determined to confront Andy. What in blue blazes was going on in this place? I left the blood-soaked room behind me, none too soon. It was starting to stink like a charnel house, especially now that Albert was well and truly dead.

I bolted into Andy's office. Andy was still sitting motionless in his seat watching the movie. I glanced at the movie screen. Perhaps it should have come as no surprise to me that the movie playing on the screen wasn't of me, but of the bloody carnage in the room I had just left.

"What the hell's going on?" I demanded. I brandished my pistol at Andy.

I would have no qualms at all about pulling the trigger and blowing away this guy, not after what I had just seen. I could not discern his face in the dark room. I could barely make out his silhouette sitting in his chair watching the movie.

I waited for an answer.

He said nothing. All I could hear was the projector humming.

"What kind of a shambles are you running here?" I said. "Let's have it, or do you want me to let *you* have it." I flourished my pistol at him again.

"Looks like I need a new number two after what you did to Albert," he said.

"Don't look at me."

"I am looking at you."

"I wouldn't take charge of this madhouse if you paid me."

He lunged out of the shadows at me with one of those green gardening trowels with metal claws that you use in a garden. In one fell swoop, he raked the steel claws across my face.

I tried to jerk my face away to avoid the blow, but not fast enough. The steel claws ripped into my flesh. I winced, anticipating the pain that would follow. Needless to say, I was surprised when there was none. Surely the claws had dug deep into my flesh when he had swiped the trowel across my face. Still, I felt no sense of pain. I felt no blood streaming down my cheeks.

"Fool," he said. "I made you just as surely as I made Albert in my own image."

He flicked the lights on. Reeling in befuddlement, I beheld his face. What passed as a face, that is. He must not have been wearing his usual makeup, his human makeup.

His real face was that of a zombie. Worm-eaten and disintegrating, his face reeked of fetid putrescence.

I flinched at the sight of him. Reflexively, I reached for my face. I tried to feel the scratches he must have inflicted on my flesh with the clawed gardening trowel. Puzzled, I did not feel skin or blood on my face. Whatever the material was felt desiccated, crumbly. There was also something rubbery mixed in with it. The rubber felt like the kind used in a latex mask. The sere substance emitted a noxious, repugnantly sweet odor. I pinched the substance between my fingers. I brought it to my eyes the better to inspect it. Its constituency reminded me of Andy's so-called face. I gagged on the now-overpowering stench of the material as it was directly beneath my nose. Disgusted, I flung the malodorous stuff on the floor and hastily wiped off any trace of it on my trouser leg. I half expected maggots to come writhing out of my face.

My God! I thought.

I, too, was a zombie.

Kiss of Death

Could it be that my realization that I was a failure drew me to her? Was I that self-centered? I had only a part-time job when we met. None of the publishers wanted the books I was writing. Maybe she would help pay the rent.

She was a waitress at a Denny's restaurant. I first saw her though the blinding rain of a January storm. Her face looked blurry like a face in a van Gogh painting. I fought my way through the rain into the restaurant. I hated the greasy tacos in the restaurant, but it was the only restaurant within walking distance of my apartment in Hollywood.

I stared at her. Her straight brunette hair was cut short at her jawline. Her apricot polyester uniform hugged her slender figure. She stuck up her nose at me.

Then I knew I would have to try my luck with her. I also felt fairly certain she would reject me. That night I said hello to her and remarked the weather. She seemed polite. I returned to the restaurant every night and spoke to her whenever she was working. She smiled a few times. I asked her out.

"I have a boyfriend," she said. "Thank you for asking."

I felt embarrassed. I gobbled my taco. I could not get out of there fast enough. I ended up with grease stains on my pants because of my nervous haste. Naturally, the stains would be on my crotch!

I analyzed my situation in my apartment. Did Wendy really have a boyfriend or did she just say that to get rid of me? She had smiled warmly when she said, "Thank you for asking." Did that mean I was OK as a friend but not as a lover?

I dreaded going back to the restaurant. I wanted her though. I had to have her. I went back two nights later to see if I could clarify our relationship—if we had a relationship.

I assertively strode into Denny's. She probably thought I would not come back to her. It was true I hated her for rejecting me. I gloated over her when I saw her, as if to say, *You didn't hurt me by rejecting me.* She looked scared. I strutted to one of her tables.

"Hi," I said.

"I'm working tonight," she said with her mauve lips. Her slender bow-shaped upper lip set off the fullness of her lower one. She averted her eyes from my steady gaze.

Why did she say that? I had not asked her out. I ate my dinner, feeling like an idiot. Was she implying that she wanted me to ask her out again, or was she telling me she did not want anything to do with me?

I did not look at her the whole time I was eating the tacos that were burning a hole in my stomach. I left without saying anything else to her. When I got home, I took an Alka-Seltzer in my apartment.

I peered into the little round mirror over the kitchenette's sink. I could not blame her for not liking me. It wasn't like I had a handsome face. The more I thought about it the more certain I was that Wendy was giving me the brush-off.

I returned to the restaurant a few days later to punish myself. Maybe I would see her with her boyfriend. I sat at a table in another waitress's section. I ate my tacos. I felt someone's eyes staring hard at me. I looked up. It was Wendy. Her big dark eyes stared at me from the other side of the restaurant. Even when I returned her gaze, she continued to stare at me.

I could not sleep that night. I kept thinking of her. If she disliked me why did she stare at me so intently? Why didn't she ignore me?

I returned to the restaurant the next night. I hesitated in the doorway. I tried to decide whether to sit in Wendy's section.

"I'm not dead," she said.

"I can see that."

I sat at one of her tables. I became excited. She must have changed her mind about us. After I finished dinner she batted her eyes at me.

"Are you doing anything tonight?" I asked.

"No."

"Do you want to go to a movie?"

"I live with my boyfriend," she said with a coy smile.

I left in confusion. If she disliked me, why was she flirting with me? I had to find out if she really lived with her boyfriend. I wanted to trail her home one night after she got off work, but she might think I was a pervert stalking her if she caught sight of me.

I asked my next-door neighbor to tail her. He was studying to become a private detective at the Nick Harris Detective School in Hollywood. He jumped at the chance. His name was Mulligan. He was in his late twenties.

"Your girlfriend's cheating on you, is that it?" he asked with cynical amusement.

"She's not my girlfriend."

Mulligan raised a smoking pipe to his hatchet face as we stood in his living room. He clicked his small teeth against the plastic pipe stem.

"Then why do you want me to follow her?" he asked.

"To see if she's living with someone."

"Is she guilty of something?"

"Not that I know of. What difference does it make?"

"I don't think I can legally hang a tail on her unless you think she's guilty of something. I would be stalking her, which is illegal."

"I'm not asking you to arrest her," I said irritably.

He glanced at a yellow brochure about mace that lay on his coffee table. "Is she dangerous?"

"No." I paused. I thought about it. "I hope not, anyway."

"Do you want photographic surveillance?"

I did not want to know what he looked like. I merely wanted to know if there was a he. "No."

"Let me get this straight. You want me to find this guy and tell you where he lives."

I nodded.

"All right," he said. "I need the experience."

"Thanks."

"I wish you wanted photographic surveillance. I just got this new digital camera with all the bells and whistles. I'd like to try it out."

"You can take pictures if you want, as long as you don't show them to me."

Mulligan grimaced. "It's not the same thing."

"Suit yourself."

"I'd have to charge you for the film if I take pictures."

"I told you, I don't want pictures."

"Don't you want to know what he looks like, so you can beat him up?"

I laughed. "Just find out if she's living with a guy."

"Two hundred dollars."

"OK," I said reluctantly. I could not afford it but I had to know about Wendy.

Mulligan wistfully eyed the 35 mm camera that sat on his deal bureau.

"I'm not paying for any pictures," I added, picking up on his gaze.

I hated the idea that she was sleeping with someone. It was only natural that she should have a boyfriend. She was sexy and pretty. She was probably flirting with me to see if I had more money than her boyfriend. In that case I had no chance with her. Or maybe it was just vanity with her. I flattered her vanity by asking her out, so she wanted me to keep asking her out. That made sense. *Vanity, vanity, all is vanity.* I had heard that before. It was a saying from the Bible.

I sat in the taco restaurant, watched her, hated her. What was so hot about her? She was lousy. She had black moles on her throat. She was pigeon-toed and had hairy arms. She disgusted me. How could I have overlooked her ugliness when I first clapped eyes on her? I felt glad she had rejected me.

She grinned lecherously at me.

"What are you doing tonight?" I asked.

"I don't know why you keep asking me out. I'm engaged."

She dropped a spoon. She leaned over to pick it up, pushing her ass at me.

If we were alone, I would have grabbed her.

I stormed out onto the sidewalk. Why *did* I keep asking her out? Maybe I wanted to fail. Maybe that was the same reason I wrote books that never got published. But I did not want to fail! If Mulligan found out she was living with someone, I would lose. If he found out she wasn't living with someone, I would still lose; it would mean she was lying to get shut of me. I should not have bothered asking Mulligan to tail her. No matter what Mulligan found out, I would lose.

Mulligan reported to me the next night. I anticipated his report with dread. Rain water was gushing down the broken aluminum drain spout at the corner of my apartment. The drain spout rattled like dishes being washed.

"I tailed her to her apartment last night," he said.

"Is she living with someone?"

"Yep."

"Who?"

"I thought you didn't want to know anything about her roommate."

"I mean, is she living with a man? She's not living with a woman?"

"It's a man."

I nodded. She had been telling me the truth about her boyfriend. I did not know whether to feel happy or depressed. She had been telling me the truth, but the truth, in this case, wasn't what I wanted to hear.

"What does he look like?" I asked. "No, forget it. I don't want to know."

"I did a little research on him. I thought you'd be interested."

"You thought wrong."

Mulligan ignored my protest. He withdrew a spiral notepad from his jacket's breast pocket. He flipped the pad's scarlet cardboard cover over to the back of the pad.

"I'm not interested," I said unconvincingly.

"He's a plumber. He's twenty-nine."

I grabbed my ears to pretend I wasn't listening, but I was. "I'm not listening."

"They've been living together for a year," Mulligan went on.

"How did you find all this out?"

"The neighbors."

He gave me Wendy's address.

"I've heard enough."

"I also snapped a picture of him."

"I told you not to."

Mulligan was annoying me with his pestering. But, I had to admit, I wanted to see the photo of Wendy's lover. Who was this guy that she preferred to me? What did he look like?

Mulligan pulled a photograph out of the rear trouser pocket of his blue jeans.

"There's a funny thing about this picture," he said, inspecting the photo.

"I don't want to see it."

I turned my head away from him. Then I turned back toward him to sneak a glance at the photo. I could not see it, not the picture anyway, just part of the back of the photograph's stock. The picture was facing Mulligan, who was standing opposite me.

Examining the photo Mulligan shook his head. "I don't understand. It must be the new camera."

"What are you talking about?"

I snagged the photo out of his hand. As much as I did not want to look at it, I had to see it.

"Is this a joke?" I snapped.

"I don't know what happened."

The photo showed the entrance to an apartment house at night. Wendy was standing alone on the cement landing.

"Where is he?" I asked.

"I don't know. I swear he was standing beside her. There must be something wrong with my new camera." Mulligan frowned. "I dropped a couple hundred bucks on that thing."

I thrust the photo back in his hand. "This isn't funny."

"It's not a joke." Mulligan scrutinized the photo again. "Maybe it's a trick of the light. Go figure."

"You can leave now."

"I'm trading this camera in. You can count on that," Mulligan said as he left my apartment.

I said good-bye. I could not understand Wendy's taste. Why did she prefer a plumber to an unpublished writer who worked part-time as a busboy at the House of Bull Dung Bar? Women made no sense.

I felt relieved she had rejected me. It meant she was faithful. If she had chosen to have an affair with me behind her boyfriend's back, what was to stop her from having other affairs behind *my* back? I wanted her to say yes to me, but I could never trust her if she said yes. *No* was the best answer but *no* got me nowhere. I had stumbled into a quandary. Whatever happened, I lost. I could not see any upside to my predicament.

The only solution was to get rid of her boyfriend. If she loved him, how could I get them to break up? Instead of worrying about her I should have been writing another book. I could not concentrate on anything with her on my mind. I hated her for making me a loser every time I asked her out. And, likewise, why should I bother writing another book that would not sell? Why did I torment myself with impossible goals? I wasn't supposed to succeed as a writer, and I wasn't supposed to succeed with Wendy. Why couldn't I get that through my thick head? Yet I refused to give up.

I drank a few beers to stop my mind from digging me into a rut. Maybe I should beat the plumber up, like Mulligan had suggested. Maybe Wendy wanted me and her boyfriend to break each other's nose over her.

What if I won the fight? How could I support her on my meager income? A pauper could not compete with a plumber. I started envying the rich and hating the rich. I hated poor scum like me. I hated everyone. I hated Wendy the most. The world jarred on my senses as though I was suffering from a hangover. The musty stench of the air made me want to vomit. Everybody was against me. I had to fight everybody. Everybody wanted me to fail.

I resigned myself to failure. How could I fight the whole world and expect to win? I should never have asked her out in the first place. But I had to try. If you wanted something or someone, you had to go for it or her. You could not be certain of anything till you tried. Afterwards you could lick your wounds. Or keep trying like I was doing and end up messing up your head.

I drove to her apartment house to say good-bye to her. We needed to hash this out so we could understand each other and move on. I spotted her place through my windshield.

She lived in a three-story avocado stucco mission-style building. A spotlight set in the front lawn and aimed at the door bathed the entrance to the lobby in green light.

I parked on the other side of the street.

I walked across the street to the apartment house. I stood on the sidewalk and watched her lighted window. Why should I bother saying good-bye to her? I did not want to confront her boyfriend. Had Wendy told him about my asking her out? I felt ill at ease standing alone in the damp darkness under the smoky plum sky in front of her apartment.

A tomcat with a fat tigerlike head and a fat tail slunk around the oleanders behind me and fell to serenading the window above us. He brushed his whiskers against the bristly watermelon red seeds.

"You too," I commiserated with him.

The tomcat's cries grated on my nerves.

"Knock it off," I whispered. "Wendy might look down here."

The moth-eaten alley cat ignored me.

I did not move in time. The ice-cold water streamed out the window above us from a pan onto my head down the back of my neck. I cringed in shock and discomfort. I stood there dripping on the cement.

The alley cat yowled and scampered into the bushes.

I realized I was going about this the wrong way.

I decided to go up to her room. I wanted to get this over with one way or the other. Enough of this pussyfooting around. My mind was made up.

I entered the lobby. Still wet, I took the elevator to Wendy's story. My damp clothes dripped onto the elevator floor as the elevator rose. The elevator stopped. Its door hummed open. I left it.

I approached Wendy's room with trepidation. She was probably going to blow me off. But I had to know how she really felt about me.

I stood in front of her door. I took deep breaths to calm myself.

I knocked on her door. Not too loud, but not too soft either. I wanted her to know that I was serious about her. I did not care if her plumber was in there with her or not. This was between Wendy and me. Was there anything happening between us? I had to know.

My heart was pumping fast in anticipation of her opening the door. There was nothing I could do about my heart's furious throbbing. It sounded so loud I thought she might hear it.

She answered the door.

"Hello," she said. She smiled at me.

"Hi. I hope I'm not disturbing you."

"No. Not at all." She noticed my wet clothes. "Is it raining out?"

"No."

"Oh. Where are my manners? Come in."

I was only too happy to oblige her.

When I entered her apartment I saw what looked like paintings in their frames standing on the carpet. They canted against the living-room wall, facing it.

A mirror was hanging askew on the same wall.

I watched Wendy approach the mirror. She was dressed in black. Her blouse was black with its two top plastic buttons unfastened. Her polyester stretch pants were black. The silk scarf around her neck was black, too.

"Can you help me?" she asked, making for the mirror.

"Sure."

"Could you move that mirror for me?" She pointed at the mirror that was hanging awry on the wall.

"No problem. Are you moving?" I grabbed the mirror.

"No. My boyfriend doesn't like mirrors. Neither do I actually." She adjusted her scarf around her neck.

I found that hard to believe—the bit about her not liking mirrors. Not with her looks. I could not imagine her not looking in a mirror at least five times a day to admire her face. That wasn't what bothered me, though. It was her mentioning her boyfriend that nettled me. I felt anger welling up inside me. There she was talking about her boyfriend again. Didn't she know it inflamed me when she talked about him? Was she trying to make me jealous?

The mirror in my hands, I held my anger in check. "Where do you want it?"

"Over there with the others."

She pointed to the objects leaning against the wall that I had mistaken for paintings.

I was about to lean the mirror against the other two when Wendy said, "The other way."

Puzzled, I looked at her.

"Face it toward the wall like the others," she explained. "You don't want seven years bad luck, do you?"

"Oh, no."

Was it seven years bad luck to face a mirror away from the wall after you removed it from the wall? That was a new one on me. Regardless, I followed her instructions. She was no doubt right. It was safer to lean it facing the wall.

"Have a seat," she said with an easy smile, gesturing toward the sofa.

I sat down.

Looking around the apartment I asked, "Where's your boyfriend?"

"He just flew out of here." She giggled.

I did not get the joke. Maybe it wasn't a joke. Maybe her giggling was some kind of sexual response to me. But was her response positive or negative? Was it ever possible to understand a woman?

"He crossed me over tonight," she added. A smile of ecstasy appeared on her face like she was lost in the transports of bliss. "I had no idea it would be like this."

I looked stunned. Was this the first time she had had sex with him? Was that what she meant by 'crossed over'? As a writer and avid reader I had encountered a spate of terms for the sexual act, but *cross over* was not one of them. I became jealous, of course.

Why was she telling me she had just had sex with her boyfriend? Did she think I cared? Was she rubbing my nose in it, trying to incite jealousy in me? It was working. She was inflaming me.

"He told me to welcome you," she went on.

Welcome me? Why would her boyfriend, a rival for her hand, want to put out the welcome mat for me? *Oh no*, I thought. Were they looking for a ménage à trois relationship? Maybe I was misunderstanding her. I hoped I was. I was a private person. I did not go in for group sex. That whole scene turned me off.

She plumped down beside me, quite close to me. Indeed, I could not help but notice that her full thigh was pressing against mine. She was pressing her whole body against mine in no time. Her subtle perfume teased my senses. I tried to identify the fragrance. It might be jasmine. I would not swear to it. The scent was too faint for me to be certain.

Her forwardness caught me off guard.

"What if your boyfriend walks in?" I asked with agitation.

"He wants what I want, and I want what he wants."

Whatever that meant. She was as cryptic as ever. I did not care what it meant. It did not matter. What mattered to me was that I was right about her, after all. When all was said and done, she wanted me as much as I wanted her.

At the same moment that she put her hand on my crotch, she plunged her vampire fangs into my jugular.

Snakebit

Radnor could not sleep. He folded his arms over his forehead. Bloodshot eyes staring, right foot restlessly working to and fro, Radnor yawned.

He had been laid off by the ad agency six months ago. Yesterday his wife had left him. He had taken up painting after he had lost his job as a copywriter. None of his paintings sold. His drinking did not help. The beers bought him a few welcome hours of forgetful sleep, but then he would wake up in the middle of the night and stay awake sweating on and off till dawn.

He had turned thirty-five last week. A year ago he had felt he had the best years of his life before him. A steady job, a pretty wife. Now this . . . He felt cheated.

That night the snake bit him. He was half-asleep when it struck his ankle under the sheets. He tore off the sheets just in time to see the black snake writhing down the mattress and under the bed. Radnor grabbed his throbbing ankle. The bite itched more than it hurt.

The snake must have escaped from the zoo down the street, he decided. He lived not far from the Los Angeles Zoo.

What kind of a snake was it? Radnor wondered. Its long forked tongue was hanging out its mouth as it fled. What kind of snake would leave its tongue dangling out its mouth?

He hopped off the bed. Gingerly, he knelt beside the bedstead. He peered beneath the bed. It was too dark. He could not see anything. He switched on the light. It was still too dark.

He had better get a move on it and see a doctor to get an antidote for the venom. He drove his car to the emergency room of the Hollywood Presbyterian Medical Center.

The young orderly in green scrubs in the emergency room gazed at him in confusion at first. The orderly's bloodshot green eyes looked like olives in martinis behind his glasses. Now the orderly was glaring at him. The man wanted to be on his way to the next patient, it seemed to Radnor.

"I don't have time to waste," said the orderly.

"A snake bit me," said Radnor. "I need a shot for it."

"Do you have insurance?"

"Yes."

"What kind?"

"Aetna."

"OK. What kind?"

"What do you mean, what kind?"

The doctor did a slow burn. "PPO. HMO. What kind?"

"HMO. Doctor, I may be dying this very minute."

"Which group are you in?"

"Group?"

"It's listed on your card," said the orderly, his patience wearing thin. "Where is your membership card?"

"In my wallet." Radnor made no attempt to retrieve it.

"May I see it?"

"What? My wallet?"

"I don't have all day. Where is your card? If you don't have a health insurance card, I can't treat you."

"*You* don't have all day? I might drop dead here in three seconds without medical treatment."

"What is your problem? Let me see your card, if you want me to proceed. I need to make sure you're in the proper group. If you're not in the proper group, you need to go elsewhere."

"What if I die before I'm able to get there?" Radnor said in exasperation.

"I'm not allowed to treat just anyone. You need to belong to the proper group."

Frustrated, Radnor gave in. As he saw it, he had no choice. He dug out his wallet from his trouser pocket. He flipped through the wallet. He located his health insurance card in its transparent plastic sheath. He extricated the card from the sheath. He handed the card to the orderly.

The orderly scrutinized it. "I don't usually do this. Usually a secretary screens a patient before I see him, but since this is an emergency—"

"Can you save me now?" Radnor chimed in.

"Wait until I find your group's name on this card." The orderly continued inspecting Radnor's card.

"Look. You must not understand. This is an emergency. A snake bit me."

"OK," said the orderly, handing Radnor's card back to him. "You're in the right group. What seems to be the problem?"

"A snake bit me. Haven't you been listening?"

"What kind of snake?"

"How should I know? I'm not a snake expert."

"I can't help you." The orderly turned to leave.

Radnor grabbed the orderly's arm. After what he had been through, Radnor wasn't about to let him go that easy. "What? Are you going to let me die just like that?"

"Different snakes have different venoms. Each venom has a different antidote. I can't give you an antidote unless I know the type of snake that bit you."

Radnor stood nonplussed. Adrenaline shot through him as he realized he was going to die.

"It was black, I think," he said. "A dark color. I could hardly see it in the night. It had a long forked tongue."

The orderly shook his head, at a loss. "I don't know a thing about snakes. You have to tell me its name. Then I'll get you the antidote."

"How am I supposed to know its name?" Radnor squawked through a tight throat.

"Well, I sure don't. Was it a rattlesnake?"

"No. It was black, or dark anyway. I didn't see a rattle on its tail."

Nurses and doctors hustled by them. A middle-aged man clutching his bleeding eye jostled Radnor. Frantic paramedics raced down the hall pushing a patient in a gurney full tilt.

I'm dying! I'm dying! Radnor wanted to say. *And there's nothing anybody can do to save me.*

"Do you feel sick?" asked the orderly.

"I feel terrible."

"What are your symptoms? Maybe we can determine the type of snake by diagnosing your symptoms."

"I feel depressed."

"Physical symptoms," demanded the orderly. "Stomachache, fever . . ."

"No. None of that."

"Maybe the snake wasn't poisonous."

"How can I be sure?"

"Identify the snake. I have work to do."

The orderly strode purposefully away from him.

"If only I had caught the snake," Radnor muttered.

An old lady with popcorn yellow hair eyed him weirdly as though he was deranged for talking to himself. She shambled by him using her walker.

Radnor had to ID the snake somehow. His laptop had crashed. He could not use that. He decided to go to the Hollywood Public Library on North Ivar Street.

He drove up to the library. It was a small, modern-looking building with a frosted-glass motif. It looked deserted. Radnor checked his wristwatch. It was too early. The library had not opened yet, he realized. He would just have to wait—as the venom worked its way through his system.

On edge, he ate breakfast at a fast-food restaurant. He felt people staring at him. Did he look like he was dying? Radnor wondered. Did they have any idea what it was like to die from a snakebite?

He finished his orange juice and coffee. He scoped out his watch. It was time to go.

He crossed the street. He entered the library. He checked the card catalog and wrote on a scrap of paper the Dewey numbers of several books on snakes.

He wove his way through rectangular deal reading tables to the open stacks. Two of the books were checked out. He could not find the third book. He cursed his luck. Haphazardly, he glanced at the

172

lower shelf. He noticed one of the snake books that he was looking for. It was out of place. He snagged it from the shelf.

He leafed through glossy pages of photographs of ugly snakes. It was impossible! he decided with frustration. There were scores of black snakes and brown snakes and grey snakes. He had not seen the snake clearly enough to remark any telltale characteristics. Maybe it wasn't black. Maybe it only looked black because of the darkness. He hung his head in dejection.

He shook his head. He could not give up. Somehow he had to try to ID the snake.

He flipped though more pages of drooling fangs and scaly iridescent skins. Snake eyes, bullet-hard snouts, sneering mouths, hissing tongues, slimy sallow underbellies . . . No dice, he decided. He would have to find the snake. Maybe it was still in his apartment.

Radnor could not believe he was still alive.

He drove to his apartment house. He rummaged through his apartment. He stripped his bed. He overturned the mattress. He inspected the bedsprings. He examined the mattress for any holes the snake might have slithered through.

He scrutinized each corner of the room. He patted the moldering rug, feeling for the snake underneath it. Clouds of dust puffed up into his face. His eyes watered. He coughed.

Entering his kitchen he flung open the cupboard under the porcelain sink. The dark empty cupboard stank of cockroach poison. He noticed the softball-sized hole in the plasterboard through which the drainpipe passed. The cockroaches entered the kitchen through the gap between the drywall and the drainpipe. The snake must have escaped through there, decided Radnor. Maybe it was in someone else's apartment at this very moment or it could be in the corridor. He had to face it. The fact of the matter was, the snake could be anywhere. He should tell the landlady.

He rifled the drawers in his bureau to make sure the snake had not taken refuge inside them. He rooted through his underwear and balled-up socks. He uncovered no snake.

A car honked on the sidewalk below his window. He looked out the window. The landlady was sitting in her green station wagon yelling for her handyman.

Radnor resumed searching his apartment. He jerked the drawers from his writing desk. He opened his paint box.

He found no sign of the snake.

The landlady honked her horn every five minutes and hollered for her handyman. Radnor wanted to scream at her to shut up! She had lost her mind, he decided. She had finally flipped. She could not take it anymore. Her husband had died last year and now she was screwy.

Radnor left his room to cast around the corridor. The faded yellow linoleum reeked of ammonia. The maid had mopped the floor yesterday. No snake that Radnor could see. The landlady pounded her horn, shrieking wildly.

Radnor searched the elevator at the end of the hall. He noticed nothing in the elevator other than its graffiti-scarred pink-painted metal walls. The air vents in the top of the left wall were big enough for the snake, Radnor realized. Maybe the snake had wriggled though the ventilation chute into the elevator shaft.

Radnor rode the elevator down to the second floor. He hunted for the snake. The landlady honked and screamed.

Radnor knocked on one of the apartment doors. A fat thirtyish man in a white T-shirt opened the door. His stubbly face gave his skin a greenish fungal appearance. He scratched his jowls. His skin rasped like sandpaper.

"Yeah?" he said.

"Did you find a snake in your room?" asked Radnor.

"Jeez!"

The green man slammed his door in Radnor's face.

The landlady honked and wailed.

Radnor opened the varnished wooden door to the staircase. The chest-high paper sign taped to the door said to keep the door closed in case of fire. Slouched in his dirt-brindled lemon coveralls in a dank corner of the stairwell was the scraggy black handyman. A blue Dodgers' baseball cap shaded his eyes. He feebly clutched a bottle of cheap whisky, spilling a droplet near his black sneaker.

"The landlady wants you," said Radnor.

"I know."

"Should I tell her you're coming?"

"No. I don't want her to find me."

"Have you seen a snake?"

"A couple."

Radnor eyes brightened. "This is urgent. I need to know where you saw these snakes."

"Crawling up the wall." The handyman pointed languorously at the wall opposite him.

Radnor saw nothing on the wall but peeling paint. "Where?"

"Right there. Don't you see them?"

"No."

"They're right there."

"This isn't a joke. If you find a snake, tell me. This is life or death. I have to find it."

"All right. How many do you want?"

Radnor descended the steps. He walked outside onto the grease-stained sidewalk toward the honking, howling landlady.

She wore a parti-colored kerchief in her sepia hair. Her broad masculine face cried out the handyman's name. Thick bright scarlet lipstick flaked off her lips. Her psychotic face reminded Radnor of a still life painted by Cezanne where the fruits on a table were portrayed from different points of view simultaneously. At least ten different countenances seemed to be vying for control of her face.

"Hi," said Radnor. "Has anyone found a snake in the apartment house?"

"Snake?" She sat in her car, giving its horn staccato taps. "Of course not. What would a snake be doing in my apartments?"

Beep-beep! Beep-beep!

"It must have escaped from the zoo."

"I hate snakes and I won't stand for them in my apartments."

Her face became increasingly masculine, Radnor noticed. Her dark eyes overflowed with poison and gorge.

"If you find it," said Radnor, "let me know. It's very important."

"Have you seen Barney the handyman?"

"No."

"Where is he?"

Her left eye roved up and down Radnor's body. She looked away. She flicked her tongue like a lizard. The tip of her tongue slid along the crusty lipstick on her lips. Then her tongue disappeared. Soon, her cheek bulged, full of tongue.

"I don't know," said Radnor. "I have to find that snake. It's life or death."

Crestfallen, Radnor returned to his apartment. He was beginning to think he would never find that snake. It could be anywhere by now.

He slumped on his tossed bed. Stuffing frothed from the mattress's slit tick. Maybe it was all a dream, he decided. Maybe he had dreamt the snake. Maybe he could not find it because there had been no snake in the first place.

He rolled down his sock to examine his ankle. A red bump rose from his ankle bone. The snake must have bitten him, he decided. Then again, maybe not. Maybe a bug had bitten him and he had dreamt it was a snake. It could have been a wish fulfillment dream. A death wish. He wanted to be dead because he had no money and Sharon had left him, so he dreamt up the snake.

If the snake really had bitten him, why wasn't he dead already? Radnor wondered.

Radnor lay back on the bed, defeated. His head ached. He felt nauseous. Maybe it was the venom doing its work, he decided. Maybe his head would burst. He was running out of options. He had no idea what to do now. This might be the last day of his life.

He heard a scraping noise on the window sill above his head. He tilted his head back to glance up. A black snake was slithering through the thick dust on the window sill, leaving behind a scalloped white trail in its wake.

Radnor jackknifed his body into a sitting position. He bolted to the kitchen. He seized a carving knife from the kitchen drawer beside the sink. Returning to his bedside he yanked open the water-stained monk's cloth drapes.

The snake flipped off the sill onto the bed. The snake coiled and uncoiled. It seemed to leap off the bed onto the carpet.

Radnor hacked at its head with the carving knife. He missed. He told himself to be calm and to keep a level head. He struck again. The snake's head fell off.

Then it wasn't a dream, Radnor decided triumphantly. The snake had been real, and he had killed it. However, he was feeling sicker and sicker by the minute. He had no time to waste. He must get to the hospital.

The snake's blood was everywhere, Radnor saw. He felt the blood drain from his face. He must hurry before he passed out.

He deposited the dead snake in a pasteboard box. He carried the box to his Ford Taurus in the garage. Behind the steering wheel he felt woozy.

He turned the key in the ignition. The car did not start. *You're kidding me!* thought Radnor. He reminded himself to stay calm. He turned the key again. He held the key in the "on" position longer this time. The engine turned over. It started.

Relieved, he put the car in gear. He used his remote to raise the garage's steel gate.

Breaking the speed limit he sped toward the zoo, still woozy, keeping his eyes peeled for the presence of police in the rearview mirror. All he needed now was to be pulled over for speeding. If the cops carted him off to the joint, he was sure he would die of the snakebite.

He screeched to a halt in the zoo's parking lot. He climbed out of the Taurus. He hauled the box with the dead snake off the front seat.

Carrying the box to the snakes' glass cages he rushed toward a young zoo attendant. She was loitering in front of one of the cages. She seemed put off by his urgency.

What did she expect? he wondered. He was about to die from a snakebite. Urgency was in order here.

"What kind of a snake is this?" he demanded.

He opened the box and shoved it under her face so she could see its contents. Damn right he was in a hurry. You would be too if a snake had bitten you, lady. Radnor could care less if she was put off by his exigent behavior.

She seemed to be frozen in time as she stood rooted to the spot, a look of sheer terror on her face.

"I'm dying!" he blurted. "It bit me. I need to know what kind of a snake it is. Help me!"

Radnor felt a frisson of fear shiver his spine. He needed the antidote for the venom. Couldn't this woman understand him? he wondered. Was she some kind of a moron?

"For Christ's sake, tell me what kind of a snake it is!" he demanded, shaking the box under her face.

She gaped at him, her blue eyes wide with dread. "That's not a snake," she managed to say.

"What is it? A giant worm? What kind of a zoo is this? Don't you people even know what a snake looks like?" He eyed the crowd that was gathering around him and the zoo attendant.

She gawked at his face. "Oh my God! Don't you know what that is?"

She was scaring the bejesus out of him. "What the hell kind of a snake is in this box!"

"It's not a snake, you poor man. It's your hand."

Confessions from the Grave

"Listen to this, Lieutenant," said rookie police officer Michael Martinelli. "It'll turn your stomach."

Forty-five-year-old Lieutenant Briscoe was just entering the room. He did not bat an eye. His wrinkled face remained fixed.

"I doubt it," he said. "I've seen it all, buddy boy." He approached the rookie. "What have you got?"

Martinelli strode across the ranch-styled mansion's well-appointed living room to an expensive stereo console on the other side of the room. He switched on the tape recorder that was hooked up to four three-foot-high walnut speakers.

"Nice setup, huh?" he said, running his eyes over the stereo with admiration.

"Music?" said Briscoe. "Is that what's supposed to turn my stomach? Must be rap music."

"A tape-recorded confession."

"Only in the Hollywood Hills," Briscoe said dryly. "In stereo yet."

"The senator must have taped it before he died from that heart attack. Heart attack in your fifties—go figure."

"Except he didn't die from a heart attack."

"What do you mean?"

"Haven't you been in the bathroom yet?"

"No."

"Then you haven't seen the corpse."

Martinelli looked puzzled. "No."

"It was no heart attack that killed him, believe me."

"Where is he?" Martinelli looked down the hallway, searching for the bathroom.

Briscoe waved him off. "Later. Who found the tape?"

"Officer Glancy. He was fooling around with the stereo, trying to play some music when he starts hearing the grisly details of this confession from hell."

"Confession to what?"

"See for yourself. I'm warning you, it's not for the squeamish."

Briscoe shook his head. He pulled a face. "Pshaw. I wasn't born yesterday."

"I actually voted for him. I thought he was a decent guy. A family man. He was all for family values."

Briscoe heard Senator Halliwell's voice emanating from the loudspeakers:

"I married my wife for her money. Her father owned a private law firm. Now Mary owns it, so we're both multimillionaires.

"She's not the best-looking flower in the garden by any means. In fact, I can't stand the sight of her. Going to bed with her is an ordeal. But I got used to it. I made believe I was with someone else, one of my mistresses. Still, I came close to vomiting every night after our 'lovemaking.'

"I had intended to divorce Mary after a few years so that I could marry a beautiful heiress and not be subjected to the torture of Mary's embrace. Mary refused to grant me the divorce.

"Perhaps it was for the best for my political ambition. Divorce can be a liability when Election Day rolls around, though nowadays it's more acceptable than it used to be.

"I racked my brains trying to figure a way to get her to grant me one. She wouldn't do it. Since she was already a millionaire many times over she cared more about the limelight than she did about the money. She loved politics because as a senator's wife she became a public figure. The media followed her every move, as well as mine. She became addicted to being the center of attention. I couldn't blame her. I knew the feeling. The fact was she was so addicted she wanted me to run for the whole shebang. The presidency of the United States.

"No wonder she hated me after I asked her for a divorce. She must have figured that I only married her for her money. No matter how much we despised each other, every time we went out in public we smiled for the cameras.

"I started going to call girls whom I met at parties. It was touch and go. I couldn't let anyone find out what I was up to or it would have meant my career. I have a reputation to uphold as a social conservative being in favor of prayer in schools and being opposed to abortion.

"I lived in a constant state of fear. What if someone found out what I was doing? What if one of the call girls tried to blackmail me? I usually went to the same one because I couldn't trust them. They knew I was a public figure and knew it would be easy to compromise me.

"This call girl Yvette seemed trustworthy—as long as I kept going to her and giving her money. If I dropped her she might turn on me. I started getting tired of her. I wanted to date another woman whom I met at a charity ball. Friends told me she was a model who was open-minded and a rich oil magnate's mistress.

"She was incredibly beautiful. I had never seen such a beautiful body and beautiful face on a woman before. Dockett, the oil magnate, told me she had been runner-up for Miss America a few years ago. He told me she lost only because her figure was a little too curvaceous for the judges' taste. What was too curvaceous for them was perfect for me.

"I've seen my share of beautiful faces and beautiful bodies. After all, as senator, I go to a lot of parties and meet a lot of people. Rarely, however, have I seen a beautiful face and a beautiful figure together on the same woman. A beautiful figure usually has an ugly face and vice versa. Though, I admit, silicone can do a lot these days to compensate for nature's frugality in the female figure department—and rich women aren't afraid of using it. Then, of course, there's always plastic surgery for the face. But this woman was a natural beauty.

"I had to have her. Her name was Cheryl. Dockett introduced me to her at one of his parties when I told him I wanted to meet her. She seemed to like me. My heart beat madly for her.

"I had to get rid of Yvette. One day I met her in the motel we used for our trysts. When I told her we should break up she started yelling. I told her to shut up. She wouldn't stop yelling and swearing.

"I seized her throat. I flung her on the bed. It felt good squeezing her throat between my fingers. She gasped and gagged. I had absolute power over her! I could crush her windpipe. I wanted to crush it!

"She writhed under me, trying with all her might to break free. 'Whore! Whore!' I snarled. Her throat made funny rattling noises.

"I released her. I backed away. She lay limp on the bed. I felt a sudden urge to stab a knife into her chest. Was I going mad? Had I killed her?

"I felt exhilarated by the triumph of my will over hers. I was the stronger. I had the right to enslave her, to kill her. I wanted to rape her as she lay dying, or was she already dead? I must have been going mad. I laughed.

"I was reaching for her dress when I heard a car pull into the motel's parking lot. Frantically, I decided I had to leave before someone found me with the corpse. I waited for the car's passengers to enter their room. I peeked through the window. I saw the guests close the door to their room behind them. I fled across the parking lot to the street curb where I had parked my car. I never parked in the motel's parking lot lest the nosy landlord might see me.

"I returned to the mansion. I was tormented by desires to rape and kill. I could still feel Yvette's throat throbbing with life under my fingers. And I liked it! I liked being able to crush the life out of her. I wanted to bash her head against the floor as well. Women were made to be raped and killed, the dirty money-grubbers. What other purpose did they serve? If you didn't kill them they'd nag you to death.

"My newfound knowledge elated me. I loved Yvette but I loved killing her even more. Murdering her gave me power, and I wanted power more than anything.

"The next day I drove to the capitol. Nobody suspected a thing. I smiled as usual. We stood around doing nothing and smiling cynically at one another, knowing we all had skeletons in our closets, thinking to ourselves, *If you try to blackmail me, I'll do the same to you.* Business as usual.

"A week later I read in the *Times* that the police had arrested a janitor at the motel for Yvette's murder. I breathed easier. That left me in the clear. I let it be known to the police chief that I wanted extra pressure brought to bear on the janitor because his hideous crime gave our state a bad name and scared the public, to boot. The media loved my performance.

"I felt empty without Yvette. I met Cheryl at another party and we started our affair that night. She knew I was worth millions. She seemed to like me, though you can never tell with women. They're such sly little liars.

"At the party I gazed fixedly at her smooth white throat. I wanted to feel it between my hands, the windpipe collapsing under my fingers. My wife was too busy posing for photographers to notice me and Cheryl sneaking glances at each other that night."

Martinelli turned off the tape recorder. "Have you heard enough? I told you it was sick."

Briscoe sighed. "Let's hear the rest of it."

"You already heard him confess to this call girl Yvette's murder."

"If there are more murders he's responsible for, we need to know. Turn it back on."

"Once is enough, as far as I'm concerned."

"How many women did he kill for Christ's sake? How many more of these do we have to listen to?"

"A bunch."

Briscoe shook his head disconsolately.

"I got sick listening to this recording just once," said Martinelli.

"This is our job." Briscoe made a circular motion with his hand, signaling the rookie to turn the cassette player back on.

"I had to promise Cheryl I loved her," Halliwell went on, "before I could get her to a motel room. Anyone can say those three little words. They mean nothing. When I was younger I used to be afraid of speaking them, as though they automatically meant marriage. But now that I was married I could say them to my heart's content without getting trapped by another woman.

"I said, 'I love you' easily now. It was no more difficult than asking the time of day. Everything became so much easier when you had money. And I had twice the money I had before I was married.

"She told me she had been gang-raped by three priests when she was fifteen. After that she felt no guilt about selling her favors.

"Our first night together I wanted to break her neck, to bend it backwards until it snapped. I felt my thumbs digging into her beautiful throat, into that flesh that glowed with health, that flesh that turned red under my thumbs. She complained that I was hurting her.

187

"'They're just love caresses,' I said.

"'You're too rough.'

"I felt her squirming beneath me. I could have snapped her neck in a second, simpler than breaking off a bird's head. 'I love you.'

"Grasping her neck I flung her head up and down against the mattress under us.

"The power! The power of life and death in my hands! It was overwhelming. I told her what I wanted from her. She wouldn't do it. Why not? She might die doing it, she said. All life was risk, I told her. Didn't she understand that? No pain, no gain. No risk, no kick. I released her throat and slapped her face. I slapped her again and again. I can't remember how many times exactly.

"I wrung her neck. I was out of my mind! I laughed. Her blue eyes bugged out of her face in abject terror. I wrapped her ginger hair tightly around her throat, yanking the ends of the locks tighter, like tying a bow.

"I finished her. I fled into the night. My feet seemed to glide over the pavement. I felt as light as air. I had to be insane! But how could I be? I'm a senator and a millionaire. Senators and millionaires don't go insane. We're role models. Everybody wants to be like us."

Martinelli turned off the tape. "What did he want her to do?"

"I don't know," said Briscoe. "I have a good idea though."

"What?"

"I think he wanted her to do what he did in the bathroom."

"Which was?"

"I'll show you after we hear the rest of the tape. Turn it back on."

"If I was mad," Halliwell continued to rant, "wouldn't they lock me in an insane asylum? I wasn't mad. Somehow I had stumbled onto the truth, the truth that nobody wanted to admit (were they afraid to admit it?): it is ecstasy to control another human being. To control him or her, body and soul. I laughed with glee. The ultimate control is murder!

"The power! The power!

"I returned to the capitol. I smiled with the rest of the politicians. I wondered if they had found out the truth too. They must have or they would not have been grinning from ear to ear.

"I looked respectable with my tie and well-groomed hair, my clean-shaven face. The photographers snapped my picture for their newspapers. That night I saw my photo on the front page of most local papers. I had cast the deciding vote on a tax bill.

"I needed another woman so I could feel the joy of power. During the week I got splitting headaches. I couldn't believe the pain.

"I knew the only thing that would make me feel better was another woman, another slender white throat crushed between my hands. Otherwise, my power drive would turn against me, depressing me.

"Everything was getting on my nerves. Backfiring cars made me jump a yard. Even someone coughing sent shivers down my spine.

"Is this what a junkie feels like when he doesn't get his fix?

"I went to a fund-raising party for my fellow party members. We all smiled and wore our best suits. Our wives wore expensive jewelry that glittered for the cameras: diamond necklaces, diamond rings, pearls, rubies, emeralds . . .

"My wife left my side the first chance she got. Truth be told, we could not stand the sight of each other, but we smiled heroically, our teeth clenched.

"I wandered around the long rectangular dinner tables until I spotted a pretty face smiling at me. Her eyes down, she let me drink in the beauty of her face. She was a gorgeous brunette with big brown eyes, doe eyes. We sneaked glances at each other for the rest of the night. My head ached but I smiled regardless.

"I got her phone number from a lawyer who was running for mayor of Los Angeles. He told me she was working for his campaign. He made it clear to me that she went above and beyond the call of duty. He winked archly and leered with one side of his mouth.

"I phoned her the day after the party. She seemed glad to talk to me. She was wealthy. Her father was a federal judge. I recognized his name immediately. One of the first laws in politics is to know the name of every politician who can help you on your climb to the top. Always be ready to give a helping hand to the pol above you.

"She had a beautiful voice. I fell in love with her over the phone. I imagined her doe eyes twinkling with desire, her breasts heaving. Her name was Diane.

"We dated. We arranged a rendezvous at a hotel. She was a little too frail for my taste. I preferred women with more meat on them, more roundness to them, healthy women who could put up a fight. Diane's throat looked like it would snap like a matchstick. But her luminous, slightly exophthalmic eyes turned me on. When I gazed into her eyes I kept wondering what she was thinking. I had no idea. She probably wasn't thinking anything.

"She confided in me that she liked dating musclemen. She once dated a muscle-bound actor but dropped him when it turned out he was gay. She found out he was dating her only for the sake of publicity. His agent had told him he needed to project an aura of heterosexuality to enhance his demand at the box office. Hence the actor dated her.

"I don't know why she told me this. Maybe she wanted to make me jealous. Some women are like that. They deliberately taunt you to make you chase them.

"She was hard to figure. She already had money, so why did she want to have affairs with married men? It wasn't the money. Then I realized it was the power of politicians that thrilled her. Like money, politics is power. Like I did, she knew the secret truth, though she had not gone far enough to see the whole truth.

"When she started telling me about a male exotic dancer she once knew, I grabbed her neck. I hurled her on the bed. My hands still locked around her neck, I straddled her chest. Power! Power! I cut off a scream in her throat. The scream turned into a long sigh. I throttled her, her mouth agape, her neck limp. I laughed my head off.

"Am I mad! Am I mad! I could have whatever I wanted in this world. Anything! I am the master! I have seen the truth and it will make you mad!

"The next day, fear took hold of me like cold steel fingers gripping my heart. I couldn't understand why I was scared. I had covered my tracks well. Nobody had seen me enter or leave the motel with Diane. But I shuddered when I walked out into the light of day, expecting someone to expose my secret.

"My guts! My guts! I'm being poisoned. Could Mary have discovered my affairs? Was she trying to poison me? Or did I simply have a stomachache?

"Depression. Blinding headaches. Futility! Nothing works. I lay in bed all day, not moving.

"I thought about killing Mary . . . No. I couldn't stand the idea of her wrinkled throat between my hands. It took away all the pleasure of killing. The more beautiful a woman is, the more joyful it is to kill her.

"I returned to the capitol. I met with other politicians. We smiled and cracked jokes then parted and stabbed each other in the back, a perpetual smile on our lips.

"Apparently I was smiling with only half my face, for I noticed men staring back at me when they saw me. Just staring at me. They weren't smiling. I also noticed women getting aroused when they saw me, flinging their eyes upward. Everybody must have wondered whether I was smiling or sneering. I wondered myself. Crooks and hypocrites. Every last one of them. What else could you do but laugh at them?

"I felt cold and hollow inside. The fear would come back and then the urge to kill. I needed a woman in my arms. The only reason I wanted power was to have a woman. That was what I used to think, anyway. Now, it seemed, the power had become more important than the woman, but women were an integral part of it because I needed to exert power over them more so than I needed to exert it over men.

"I went for a month without finding any lookers. I thought about phoning a call girl, but you could never tell what you were getting when you asked for one, sight unseen. I was sure something would turn up—beautiful women with a price tag gravitated toward power—but I couldn't wait.

"I drove to a cathouse in Hollywood. Could I be insane and not know it? Lunatics don't know they're mad.

"She had an incredible body. I had to be careful no one recognized me at the cathouse. That's the problem with being a public figure . . ."

"The tape ends there," said Martinelli.

"He's almost got me convinced," said Briscoe.

"Convinced?"

"That he's not mad."

"I think I'm gonna be sick."

"I wish we had found this tape sooner. We might have saved a few women's lives."

"To think a madman was our senator."

Briscoe smiled wryly. "If it wasn't so horrible, it would be funny."

"Now what about his death? You said he didn't have a heart attack."

"Follow me."

Martinelli followed Briscoe to the bathroom.

Briscoe stopped in the bathroom's doorway. "Don't toss your cookies," he said, looking into the bathroom.

"If I didn't do it listening to that sick tape, I won't do it now," Martinelli assured him.

"Take a gander at that, then." Briscoe walked into the bathroom.

Martinelli stepped into the doorway. As Briscoe moved out of the way, Martinelli could see the shower stall.

Martinelli ducked. He grabbed the toilet and promptly threw up.

Halliwell was hanging by the neck from a leather belt that was fastened to the showerhead. He was naked, save for another leather belt buckled around his waist. The bottom of the white porcelain bathtub was covered with pornographic photographs in living color. But Halliwell wasn't living. His face was blue, his body was naked, and he was holding his penis in his hand. He was also quite dead.

"Give me a break," muttered Martinelli into the toilet. His voice echoed back into his face.

"Autoerotic asphyxiation, that's what they call it. Halliwell was looking for the biggest kick of all."

"What the hell was he trying to do?" Martinelli wiped bits of vomit off his face with the back of his hand.

"Haven't you ever heard of *autoerotic asphyxiation*?"

"No."

"He was trying to have an orgasm while strangling himself to death."

"People do that?"

Briscoe nodded. "The idea is to release the noose around your neck as you come."

Martinelli rolled his eyes. He shook his head. "Different strokes . . ."

"It's supposed to double your pleasure. Halliwell was having so much fun he forgot to release the noose. Just as well. Saved the taxpayers some money on using Old Sparky." Briscoe cleared his throat. "I mean, saved some money on a lethal injection. Never could understand why they got rid of the chair in California." He looked with disgust at Halliwell's naked corpse hanging from the showerhead. "The papers are gonna have a field day with this."

The Invisible Enemy

McGill sat on an aluminum-framed lawn chair on the narrow balcony of his dilapidated apartment house in the quiet California seaside town of Almara. He smoked a cigarette. The ash fell on the rusted metal banister in front of him. He suddenly flinched and clutched the aluminum armrests of his chair, dropping his cigarette.

He leaned forward, his body tense with fear. But then he wondered why he should be afraid. By now he should be used to it. It had been happening like this all year long.

He watched a pedestrian, Almara's seventysomething pharmacist Ed Burton, get run over by a weaving station wagon that swerved across the solid double yellow lines into him. The pedestrians on the opposite sidewalk did not even bat an eye. Their black stone eyes stared straight ahead all the while, not noticing anything or not caring or both, decided McGill.

McGill should be used to it by now after a year, he knew, but no matter how many times he saw it, he could not ignore it like everybody else. He expected it to happen on a daily basis, but he was not dead to it like the others.

Now McGill watched the twisted body of Burton as he lay on the street, broken. His face swollen, his right arm twitching, Burton grimaced in agony. It was no surprise to McGill, but a shock to his system, nonetheless, when the station wagon shrieked to a stop. McGill figured he knew what was going to happen next. He was right. The station wagon made a three-point turn, doubled back toward Burton, and ran him over again. The car rose in the air, tipping upward on its left, as its left front tire rolled over the length of Burton's body. Then its left rear tire ran over him as well. Blood squirted out of Burton's mouth as the heavy car's tires ground him into the pavement.

McGill could not bear looking at it. He shut his eyes. The other pedestrians just kept walking, not even breaking stride. The station wagon's rear tires shrieked on the pavement as soon as the left rear tire grabbed the asphalt after the car had finished crushing Burton. The car fishtailed and careered away down the coast highway.

It had not always been like this, McGill knew. Only for the past year had things in Almara gone to hell. The entire city had turned into a lunatic asylum.

McGill had resigned from his job in protest a year ago because his boss at the security company had cut back his hours and would not pay him enough to live on. Ever since then, McGill spent his time sitting daily on his balcony and watching the people below on the sidewalks and on the beach.

He watched them body-surf and cavort in the ocean's breakers. Teenagers rode their skateboards in the beach's parking lot. Joggers jogged through the warm sand. Sometimes drinking a beer, McGill would watch it all, feeling life was passing him by.

After he had left his job, he lived on his life savings and pretty much kept to himself. And maybe his solitude was what had saved him from the enemy that was laying siege to Almara. Maybe, he decided, the enemy had not gotten to him yet because McGill's penchant for solitude prevented the disease from spreading from its victims to him. In effect, he was in self-imposed quarantine.

The enemy struck down the poor people and the old people first; the rich, the teenagers, and the politicians seemed to last the longest, McGill had noticed.

When McGill's brother had died two weeks ago, Dr. Weller had explained the symptoms at his bedside. Sporting a shock of white hair, Weller was spindle-legged with a game leg that he had got playing wide end at the University of Southern California. He had peered over his half-moon glasses at McGill, as McGill's older brother Anthony was stretched out dead on the bed beside them.

"First your eyes go dead," Weller had said. "Then you start moving slower than you used to. You become indifferent. You don't eat much. Then one day you stand still, you don't move for an hour, you sit down, and you die twelve hours later."

"How does that fit in with all the crazy stuff people are doing like running each over without caring one way or the other?" McGill had asked.

Weller had nodded. "That's the indifference. You just do whatever you want, not caring what happens."

"What causes it?"

Weller had removed the stethoscope from his neck. He had placed the stethoscope inside his medical bag. "We don't know yet."

"Is it a disease?"

"It must be, but we can't identify it." Weller had shaken his head. "Even the CDC back east can't determine the pathogen." He had hitched toward the door, breathing heavily. His black medical bag swung out at his side.

"The Centers for Disease Control?"

"You got it." Weller had smiled and winked at McGill.

"Is the disease contagious?"

"Highly."

"I suppose I'm next then."

"Not necessarily. We don't know how it's passed—whether it's by air or by food. We just don't know."

"But I was with him when he died."

"So was I. I've been with scores when they died."

"How can we prevent—"

"We can't prevent a thing, till we know the cause," Weller had barked, his nerves on edge from overwork.

"It's hopeless, isn't it?" McGill had said tonelessly.

"We're not licked yet. As long as we can breathe we can fight. Science can solve any problem."

"But how can we fight something when we don't even know what it is? How do you fight an invisible enemy, Doc?"

Weller had not said anything. He had left the apartment in silence.

McGill knew he would have to phone Anthony's wife, who was a reporter working as a stringer for a newspaper in San Francisco, and tell her about Anthony's death. McGill kept putting it off.

He felt frustrated. It was the same way he had felt when he looked for another job and could not find one. Who was doing this to him? he wondered. Why was it happening?

Sitting on the balcony now, he heard footsteps. He turned his head. He saw Lieutenant Spencer of the local police force. Spencer was dressed in a butternut uniform. He was climbing the salt-eroded wooden steps to McGill's balcony. Spencer reached McGill's side. Spencer stood there. Spencer grasped the balustrade. He peered over it at Burton's motionless, pulpy corpse on the street below. Burton's thick blood was coagulating on the asphalt. There was a metallic sheen to the crimson blood that was turning gradually brown.

"Did you see it happen?" Spencer asked McGill.

"A station wagon ran him over."

"How did it happen?"

"The station wagon weaved over the double yellow lines and struck him."

"The driver must have been drunk. Did you get the license plate?"

"It was too far away." McGill paused. "Then the station wagon drove back and ran over Burton again."

Spencer eyeballed McGill. "If that's the case, it was coldblooded murder."

"Or maybe the enemy did it."

"What enemy?" asked Spencer, his brown eyes fixed on McGill's face. The tips of Spencer's long sideburns extended nearly to the edges of his mouth.

"The enemy that's killing the whole town."

Spencer cocked an eyebrow. "You mean the disease."

"Whatever it is."

"We can't blame everything on that."

"A bunch of witnesses saw the whole thing and paid no attention to it."

"That even happens when people are healthy."

"Nobody gawked either. Nobody paid any attention to it. They just kept walking along."

"What do you want me to do about it, McGill?" Spencer ground his teeth.

"I don't know."

Hands clenching and unclenching, Spencer descended the balcony's wooden steps. He walked in a tight circle on the ground, his head down. He returned to the balcony's stairs. He looked up at McGill.

"The pressure's getting to me," said Spencer.

"There's nothing you can do about it. It's not your fault."

"You're just a bum. What do you know?"

"Not by choice."

"I can't stand sitting back and letting our whole town be wiped off the map. I want to fight this thing!"

"How?"

Spencer ran the fingers of his left hand through his hair. He screwed up his face. "I don't know. There must be something we can do."

"Wait it out," suggested McGill.

"No! How can you be so damned indifferent? Maybe you already have this disease." Spencer eyed McGill suspiciously.

"I'm not indifferent. I want to do something as much as you. But what?"

"We've got to do something. Anything. We can't give up." In disgust Spencer watched another car run over Burton's corpse, not even bothering to slow down or steer around it. "Jeez! First off, we've got to get that body out of the road. What's happening, McGill? Are we all going nuts?"

"Happens to the best of us," said McGill, attempting a lame joke that Spencer did not appreciate.

Spencer stared at McGill like he was a bug impaled on a pin.

Then Spencer laughed, recalling that his was the life of a cop. This was the type of thing, like rape and murder, that cops dealt with on an everyday basis. The only way he could get through it was by having a sense of humor, he knew, even if it was gallows humor.

"What's a little plague among friends?" he said through his laugh.

"Want to bet who lasts longer? You or me?"

Spencer sneered. He clumped up the balcony's steps. Bunching his fist he punched McGill's shoulder. The blow drove McGill stumbling backward. He fetched up against the balustrade. He leaned backwards over it thanks to the impetus of Spencer's punch. McGill managed to catch himself in time before he toppled to the sidewalk below. He straightened up.

"I want to kill that disease," Spencer snarled. "I have to fight it somehow."

McGill massaged his throbbing shoulder. "What good is killing me going to do?"

Spencer shrugged. "I had to hit someone. You happened to be around." He retreated down the steps.

"We wait till we can figure out what we're up against here. Then we attack it."

Spencer waved the back of his hand disdainfully at him. "Coward . . . No wonder you don't have a job."

His Parthian shot goaded McGill. McGill knew he was no coward. If he was a coward he would have fled town a long time ago.

He watched Spencer drive off in his squad car, no doubt to retrieve paramedics to help remove Burton's body from the street.

A murder of crows blackened the sky overhead as they swooped down and alighted on the catenary telephone wires that stretched from the poles alongside of the road. Two dirty white track shoes that were tied together with their shoelaces were hanging from the middle of one of the wires. Perched on the wires, the hungry crows eyed the corpse in the road.

From his balcony McGill watched the crows. They looked like they were on the verge of dive-bombing Burton. Awaiting the spectacle, McGill scoped out Burton's smashed, broken corpse.

McGill could not believe what he was seeing. Nonplussed, he watched Burton use his arm and jack himself to a sitting position on the asphalt.

The crows must have realized their error, decided McGill. Filling the air with the beat of their fluttering wings, they dispersed, darkening the overcast sky. The crows wanted none of it.

McGill shook his head, trying to clear his eyes, which must have been deceiving him. This could not be happening, he knew. He had seen Burton run over twice by a vehicle that must have weighed close to a ton. And then Burton had been run over again a few minutes ago.

Nevertheless, McGill watched transfixed as Burton dragged his pulpy, misshapen body to his

Bryan Cassiday

feet. Burton spotted McGill watching him. Burton began limping toward McGill. Burton's body looked grotesque, what with its broken arms and legs sticking out at all angles. Indeed, Burton could barely hobble on his broken legs.

McGill realized Burton had a fixed look in his glassy eyes and those eyes were staring right at McGill.

McGill shook himself out of his stupor. He left the balcony and entered his apartment. He made for his closet. He opened it. He pulled out a double-barreled over-and-under twenty-eight gauge Mossberg shotgun with a twenty-six inch barrel. Living by himself he did not trust anyone. He kept the Mossberg on hand for self-defense. He reached onto the top shelf in the closet. He pulled down a cardboard box of number six lead-shot shells for the shotgun.

He withdrew two red plastic cartridges from the box. He snapped open the shotgun. He inserted a cartridge into one chamber of the shotgun. He was about to insert another cartridge into the next chamber when he thought he heard somebody climbing the steps to his apartment. He fumbled the cartridge to the floor in his haste to load the shotgun.

He reached for the box of shells on the shelf. He pulled out another shell. He inserted it into the shotgun. He straightened out the broken-open shotgun as he snapped it shut.

Hearing the wooden steps creaking on his balcony's stairway, he carried the shotgun to the balcony. He cocked one of the triggers. He stole toward the balcony.

He surveyed the balcony. It was deserted. He walked onto it. He checked out the stairs. He saw

Burton lurching up the steps, barely able to move his contorted limbs.

"Get out of here or you're dead!" McGill warned. He brandished the shotgun at Burton.

Burton paid no attention to him. Burton grunted. He kept limping up the steps. To McGill, the grotesque-looking Burton looked like he was dead already.

Well, Burton would just have to die all over again, McGill decided. McGill trained the shotgun on Burton.

"I'm warning you, Ed," said McGill. "I mean business."

No dice. Burton kept hobbling up the steps. He was getting a little too close for comfort, McGill decided.

McGill let him have it. He blasted Burton in the chest. The shot resounded over the beach. Burton could not have been more than six feet away from McGill. The lead shot blew apart Burton's chest. Burton reeled backward, stumbling down two steps. Grabbing the handrail he managed to keep his balance. Incredibly, he started climbing the steps toward McGill again.

McGill watched Burton in awe. How could Burton survive a direct hit of number six lead shot from a twenty-eight gauge shotgun to his chest? McGill wondered. At point-blank range, no less.

McGill cocked the other barrel. This time he trained the shotgun's barrels on Burton's head. He squeezed the trigger. The lead shot practically tore Burton's head off his neck. Burton's brains were pulverized. His head dangled on his shoulder from what was left of his decimated neck. Burton collapsed. He rolled down the rest of the steps. He fell in a heap on the cement landing. He lay motionless.

McGill could not believe what he had just witnessed. There was no way Burton could have survived being run over. Maybe if he had been run over just once, he might have been able to survive. But not twice and yet again after that. McGill had seen two wheels run directly over Burton's rib cage the second time Burton was run over. Burton's heart had to have been crushed. And how could Burton survive a point-blank shotgun blast to his chest?

Maybe this was the second phase of the disease, decided McGill. The first phase was indifference followed by death. The second phase could be a reanimated corpse. McGill hoped he was wrong. But if he was, he would have a lot of explaining to do to Spencer—like how did Burton get a load of lead shot in his chest?

McGill watched Burton for a full minute and change, making sure Burton was dead this time.

McGill heard a knock on his apartment's door. He retreated into the living room. He crossed the circular path that was worn in the shag carpet where he regularly paced the room. He stowed the shotgun in the closet. A cockroach scampered across the carpet, scuttling too fast for McGill to stomp it.

McGill wasn't used to having guests. He had already had two today if you counted the zombie Burton. Now McGill had a third. He opened the door.

Anthony's wife Brigitte confronted him, her eyes swimming.

"I got back an hour ago and I found out what happened—to Tony," she said.

Her big blue eyes looked luminescent as they were welling with choked-back tears. Along with her shapely eyebrows, her eyes aroused McGill. He had not been with a woman since he had lost his job. His arousal was fleeting though. He was still mortified from having watched Burton rise from the dead.

"Come in, Brigitte."

Entering, she glanced in disgust at two roaches that scurried across the carpet.

"They're angry because they haven't been fed," said McGill, noting the direction of her gaze. "The cute little devils."

"Your brother is dead and you're cracking jokes?" She gave him a look.

"What am I supposed to do? Cry for a week?"

"At least show a little compassion, as though maybe you cared about him." She sobbed. Sniffling, she dredged a handkerchief out of her pocketbook, dabbed her nose with the silk, and closed her eyes.

"There's nothing we can do for him now."

Brigitte surveyed McGill's apartment. She took in the peeling paint on the walls, the bureau covered with a thick layer of dust, the broken plaster in the water-stained ceiling where the rain leaked through the roof, the crumpled balls of Kleenex on the floor, the drawn-shut faded khaki drapes.

"How can you stand living here?" she asked.

"I like a good joke."

"It's not funny. It's sad."

"I guess I better not ask you to stay."

"Are you still writing?"

He turned away from her. "No. I'm never going to write another word."

She smiled briefly. "You always say that before you start writing."

"There's no money in it. Why should I bother? How about you?"

"I write only for the paper. I would never write fiction."

"Why not?"

"I'm afraid of making a mistake. The book might not come out right. It might not say what I want it to say."

"Did you ever hear of rewriting? You know what Hemingway said. The first draft is always shit."

"Why should I listen to you? You quit writing."

He shrugged. "I have to worry about paying the rent."

"You don't look very worried." She studied his face, his fine features, his enigmatic eyes that never gave themselves away.

It was clear to McGill that she felt annoyed she could not get through to him.

"I don't think you understand what's going on in this town," he said.

She replaced her handkerchief in her purse. "What's that supposed to mean?"

He debated whether he should tell her about the zombie Burton. He decided she would not believe him. "Nothing."

She shook her head. "All you ever think about is yourself. I guess you won't be coming to Tony's funeral."

"Tell me when it is and I'll be there." He stepped toward her, stood by her side, and gazed at her face. Her eyes still seemed to be swimming in tears.

"What?" she said, noticing him staring at her.

"I haven't seen tears in this town for a long time."

"You mean everybody's like you now."

"No. The enemy's got them."

"Enemy?"

"The doctor calls it a disease."

"The disease that killed Tony?"

McGill nodded.

"I read about this disease when I was in San Francisco," she said. "Hundreds of people are suddenly dying in Almara and nobody knows why."

"So what else is new?"

"I need to find out more about it."

"We all do, or it'll be the end of us."

She hung on his words. "What's that mean?"

"It means the disease is killing us all off."

The journalist in her answered him. "This sounds like a good story."

McGill thought about it. "I'd like to describe the invisible enemy in a short story."

"How can you describe something that's invisible?"

"It's impossible, but it would be a challenge."

"You must want to be a failure. You got what you wanted." She spread her arms, gesturing to his unkempt apartment. She raised her shapely eyebrows to emphasize her words.

As much as he hated to admit it, she had a point. After all, if he wasn't going to write anymore, it was tantamount to being a failure.

Brigitte opened the door and walked out. Her high-heel leather boots clacked against the hallway's linoleum tiles. He could not help but notice her sheer skirt swinging across her haughty hips.

McGill stepped to the doorway. He watched her depart with a tinge of regret.

She disappeared down the stairwell at the end of the hall. McGill was about to close his door when, moments later, a man with his head bent forward emerged from the stairwell at the other end of the corridor. He was rocking his head from side to side. Yet another guest today, decided McGill. It was Lieutenant Spencer, McGill realized. Spencer came toward him trudging down the hall, muttering.

"Nobody can escape it," said Spencer. "A hundred more dead . . . my wife . . . I can't deal with it."

Unseeing, he entered McGill's apartment and jostled his shoulder into McGill's. Spencer did not apologize. He did not seem to realize what he had done. He plodded past McGill into McGill's apartment.

McGill could not fathom what was going on with Spencer. Spencer looked out of it. Fists clenched, paying no attention to McGill, Spencer made a beeline for the balcony. McGill followed him.

"What's the matter?" asked McGill.

"What's the point? It's hopeless," Spencer said without turning to face him. "We'll never find out what's doing this to us. What's the point?"

"It's how you meet the pressure that counts."

"By doing nothing—like you?"

McGill took umbrage at Spencer's dig. "Should I run around like a chicken with its head cut off? What good will that do?"

"We have to do something." Spencer bobbed his head and muttered something unintelligible that McGill could not catch.

"We have to be patient and ready to fight when the time comes."

McGill eyeballed Spencer with concern. Spencer wasn't himself, that was for sure, decided McGill. What was Spencer gibbering about?

"I can't stand the waiting," said Spencer.

"You can't fight what you can't see."

"My wife is dead! Can't you understand?" Spencer gripped his head between his hands, his eyes shut.

McGill sighed in frustration. "So is my brother."

Spencer climbed onto the balcony's balustrade. Before McGill knew what he was doing, Spencer leapt off the balcony. McGill sprang to the balustrade to stop him. As McGill bounded across the balcony, he could see it was too late. He saw Spencer's limp body falling through the air at a slight angle away from the building. Spencer crashed into the sidewalk facedown.

Even from the height of his balcony McGill could hear the nauseating crack of Spencer's skull.

Two grey-haired women shambling on the sidewalk sneaked glances at Spencer's body that sprawled before them. They looked away stonily, their heads down. They carefully walked off the sidewalk to avoid stepping on the oozing bits of Spencer's brain matter splattered on the cement. Their faces displayed no emotion save for a mild annoyance that they were obliged to leave the sidewalk to pass the corpse. As for Burton's corpse at the foot of McGill's staircase, they showed no reaction to indicate that they had even seen it.

McGill knew the enemy had the two women in its death grip. Likewise, McGill knew the enemy had under its sway the ambulance driver who was just now hurtling his ambulance past the corpses without braking. Looking at Spencer, McGill realized with a turn: if the enemy did not destroy you, you ended up destroying yourself—like Spencer.

A scrub jay squawked in a palm. Cars rushed by sounding like waves crashing on a desolate strand.

His stomach knotted, McGill backed off the balcony into his room. He heard someone knocking at his door. He hoped it was Brigitte. He opened the door. It wasn't Brigitte. It was his brother Tony.

Taken aback, McGill watched Tony with awe.

Tony opened his mouth in the hallway. His breath smelled like formaldehyde. Maybe it was embalming fluid, McGill figured. Tony grunted. He raised his hand and grabbed McGill's shoulder. His mouth still open, Tony started to yank McGill toward him.

McGill broke away from Tony's grasp. This wasn't Tony, McGill knew. Tony was dead. McGill had been there when Doctor Weller had pronounced Tony dead. McGill darted for the closet that contained his shotgun. He wrenched open the closet door. He snagged the Mossberg. But Tony was right behind him, grunting, stumbling after him, groping for him like a monomaniacal blind man.

McGill did not have time to load the shotgun. Instead, he wheeled around and clubbed Tony in the head with the shotgun's wooden stock. Tony groaned but kept coming. McGill must not have clubbed him hard enough. He kicked Tony in the stomach and tried to shove him away. Tony staggered backwards a few steps.

McGill burst into the closet. He snaked his hand to the top shelf to retrieve the box of ammunition. As he pulled down the box he dropped it. Red cartridges spilled onto the floor. He cursed. He bent over. He snatched up one of the cartridges that were rolling on the floor near his foot. He stamped his foot on the cartridge to stop it from rolling any farther.

Tony was coming at him again.

McGill figured he just needed one cartridge. He wasn't even going to bother loading two shells into the shotgun's chambers. He knew he had no time to spare.

His mouth hanging open, Tony grabbed McGill's arm. McGill had not finished loading the shotgun. He could not shoot Tony. McGill jammed the shotgun's barrel into Tony's stomach. Tony kept coming. McGill kicked Tony in the stomach again.

Tony staggered backward. He windmilled his arms as he tried to catch his balance.

While kicking Tony, McGill lost his grip on the broken-open shotgun. The shotgun clattered to the floor. McGill retrieved the shotgun. He jammed a cartridge into the shotgun's empty chamber. He saw Tony coming toward him again. McGill snapped the shotgun shut. He fired directly at Tony's ashen, wizened face. In fact, the muzzle was so close to Tony's face it was touching his mouth.

The lead shot blew Tony's face apart. His head exploded into blood-soaked spalls of gleaming white skull and brain matter. They pasted the ceiling and nearby wall. Some of the shards got on McGill's face. He brushed away the bloody fragments on his face and mouth with the back of his hand.

McGill could not stand the sight of his mutilated brother any longer. McGill flung the bloody-barreled shotgun down. He bolted toward the balcony. He scrammed down the stairs two steps at a time to the sidewalk. He needed to get out of that room. He could not cope with his memory of having blown away his own brother— even if Tony had already been dead in the first place when McGill had blasted him. McGill needed air. He needed to put as much distance as possible between him and his apartment that had turned into an abattoir.

At the foot of the stairs he saw Burton's corpse. Ten-odd feet away from it lay Spencer's. McGill paused for only a second to take them in. Then he beat it.

He kept going, not walking but not running either. He was striding like a businessman late for a meeting. If he started running, he feared lest bystanders might become suspicious of him. The last thing he wanted to do was draw attention. He did not want to look like he was running scared or like he was running away from something.

The sun broke through the overcast sky, which was filmy and swirling like grey milk in water. The sun spilled light over the palm fronds and onto the pavement. The sunshine felt good on his face, but nothing had changed, McGill knew—the invisible enemy was still wiping out the town like the plague that it was.

At a newspaper vending machine he paused to read the headlines through the transparent plastic lid: even the rich, the young, and the politicians were dying now.

He loitered down the sidewalk. He needed to determine what to do next. He made for a rare pay phone on the sidewalk. He did not own a cell phone because he had no one to call. Besides, cell phones were expensive. He lifted the handset on the pay phone. He inserted quarters into the coin slot. He phoned paramedics. He told them Spencer had fallen off his balcony.

McGill hung up.

He resumed walking. Three pallid-faced young men in grey suits walked past him. They had flat, dead eyes. McGill sighed. More infected people, he decided.

The disease seemed to be spreading much faster now, which had a grim sort of logic to it. If ten persons had the disease, it stood to reason they would spread it ten times faster than one person would. Every person was different though. The person with the most social contacts would spread the disease faster than a recluse would. McGill, a virtual hermit, figured that that was the reason he still had not contracted the disease.

McGill decided to visit Doc Weller at his home. McGill had no idea who else to turn to.

Reaching Weller's pricy bungalow on foot, McGill knocked on the door. Weller opened it, scratching his shock of white hair. As he opened his mouth, incoherent words passed through his lips. His eyes vacant, he seemed to see McGill. McGill wasn't sure. Weller grinned, his eyes focused on nothing.

"Is anything the matter, Doc?" asked McGill.

Weller mumbled. None of his words sounded intelligible.

"Lieutenant Spencer . . . he's—dead," said McGill.

"Yayayaya," said Weller.

"Did you find out if the enemy is a disease?" McGill eyed Weller's face suspiciously.

"Nanynananana . . ."

The instant he realized Weller had lost his mind McGill figured the cause: Weller's scientific intelligence had failed to identify the enemy and, unable to cope with the impotence of his intellectual powers, he had gone mad.

McGill could not bear the sight of the shell of a man who was grinning like a maniac in front of him. Weller had once been a brilliant doctor. Now he was a babbling idiot. McGill figured Weller was entering the first phase of the disease.

McGill fled from the bungalow down the driveway onto the street. At this point he did not care if anybody saw him running. They were all probably infected with the disease anyway, he decided. None of them cared about anything. Why would they give a damn about a running man? Where could he turn now? he wondered.

The invisible enemy was ravaging everybody. He told himself to remain calm, to meet the pressure with a cool head.

Sprinting down the street, he collapsed after running several miles. He fought off his exhaustion. He struggled to pull himself to his feet.

Gasping, bent forward, palms on thighs, he knew he could not fight an enemy he could not identify. He realized he could do but one thing. He must tell everybody he met about the danger humanity faced. Even if they could do nothing to protect themselves, even if they locked him away in a madhouse, it was best they knew they were under attack.

Otherwise, there was no hope of defeating the invisible enemy.

He would write a description of the disease's symptoms and send letters to every newspaper in the country. Maybe then someone could find a cure, and if nobody did and everybody told him he was wasting his time, he would go on trying to tell the world about the enemy—until the enemy took him, too.

www.ingramcontent.com/pod-product-compliance
Lightning Source LLC
Chambersburg PA
CBHW060435180626
46817CB00007B/2819